"Kidnapping is

"Kidnapping? Is that what y

"What would you call it?"

"Returning a favor. You saved my life. Now I'm doing the same for you."

"It's hard to believe that's what you're doing when you're pointing a gun at me."

"Sorry." Hawke tucked the gun into his jeans.

Miranda eyed the man, the car door, the traffic speeding by. Maybe—

"Whatever you're thinking, forget it."

Miranda stiffened, turning to face him again. "I'm not thinking anything."

"Sure you are. You're thinking about opening the car door and jumping for it. Or maybe attracting someone's attention." Hawke shrugged. "It's what I'd do if I were in your position."

"And if I were in your position, I'd stop the car and let my prisoner out." Miranda tried to sound less scared than she felt.

"You're not a prisoner."

"Then what am I?"

"The newest member of the witness protection program."

Books by Shirlee McCoy

Love Inspired Suspense

Steeple Hill Trade

SHIRLEE McCOY

has always loved making up stories. As a child, she daydreamed elaborate tales in which she was the heroine—gutsy, strong and invincible. Though she soon grew out of her superhero fantasies, her love for storytelling never diminished. She knew early that she wanted to write inspirational fiction, and began writing her first novel when she was a teenager. Still, it wasn't until her third son was born that she truly began pursuing her dream of being published. Three years later she sold her first book. Now a busy mother of four, Shirlee is a homeschool mom by day and an inspirational author by night. She and her husband and children live in Maryland and share their house with a dog and a guinea pig. You can visit her Web site at www.shirleemccoy.com.

VALLEY OF SHADOWS

Shirlee McCoy

Steeple
Hill®

Published by Steeple Hill Books™

STEEPLE HILL BOOKS

Steeple
Hill®

ISBN-13: 978-0-373-44251-5
ISBN-10:   0-373-44251-3

VALLEY OF SHADOWS

Copyright © 2007 by Shirlee McCoy

www.SteepleHill.com

Printed in U.S.A.

This is what the Lord says: "Stand at the crossroads and look; ask for the ancient paths, ask where the good way is, and walk in it."

—*Jeremiah* 6:16

To Jude—musician, budding scientist, young man of God. May the path God has set for you be clear, may your faith be strong and may you always know just how much I love you and just how proud I am to be your mother.

To Jeannine Case. Piano teacher extraordinaire. Thank you for all the years of hard work and dedication you've given to your craft. May every day, every moment be filled with joy and every memory one to cherish.

To Ms. Dawn of Docksiders Gymnastics in Millersville, Maryland, who gives children wings and teaches them to fly. What you do really does matter.

And to Melissa Endlich. Editor. Cheerleader. Conference buddy. I promise I'm not going to say one more word about redheads, or knights or even accountants! Maybe.

ONE

The warm September day had turned chilly with sunset, the brisk air heavy with approaching rain. Miranda Sheldon shivered as she stepped outside of her three-story town house, goose bumps rising on her bare arms as clammy coolness seeped through her cotton T-shirt. A jacket would have been a good idea, but she'd been in a hurry to escape the house. Grabbing one had been the last thing on her mind and, as much as she knew she'd probably regret it, she wouldn't return for one now. Not when her sister Lauren was there.

And not when memories filled every corner, sorrow every silent room.

Instead, she moved quickly, setting a rapid pace, hoping it would warm her as nothing else had in the past few days. People milled around her as she hurried down the busy Essex street. Many she recognized as patrons of the small bakery she owned. A few called out to her, some offering quiet condolences before moving on to whatever they'd planned for Friday night. Their words echoed in her ears, whispered through her head and lodged in her throat, nearly choking her with their potency. Comfort, sympathy. She wanted neither. What she wanted was to rewind the clock, to change the past, to make different choices that would lead to different outcomes.

But, of course, she couldn't do any of those things. All she could do was grieve and move on with a life that seemed empty and void.

Two blocks down and around a corner, the neighborhood grew quiet, the sounds of traffic and voices muted, the busy Maryland town hushed. Miranda hesitated at the top of a cul-de-sac, the darkness not able to hide the truth of where her walk had taken her. Not just any street. Not just any place. This was where she'd spent the better part of two days. A place where she'd greeted those who'd come to share her sorrow. A place that she'd be happy to walk away from and never see again.

Earlier, the lawn of the huge Greek revival had gleamed brilliant emerald in the sunlight. Now, it was a blanket of shifting shadows, the half-bare trees that lined the driveway skeletal. Light glowed from the lower level of the building, but the remainder of the house was dark, the tall windows eerie in the moonlight. At night, more than any other time, Green's Funeral Home looked like what it was—a place for the dead.

Miranda shivered, but moved forward anyway, knowing that she couldn't turn back now. She hadn't planned to come, but she was here and maybe it was for the best. If someone was still working at the funeral home, she might get a chance to say a final goodbye. A *private* goodbye. It was the last opportunity she'd have before the burial. She couldn't pass it up.

The foyer of the building was brightly lit and visible through the panes of glass on either side of the door. Miranda knocked, then twisted the knob. It was locked as she'd expected, the funeral home empty. She should go home, finish the baking she was doing for the funeral and check over the list of things that had to be ready before tomorrow. That was the practical thing to do. But with her nephew Justin gone, practical didn't seem quite as important as it once had been. Nor did home seem the comfortable place she'd thought it to be. Maybe once Lauren returned to her work and travels, Miranda could return to the quiet life she'd built for herself.

Maybe, but she didn't think so. Her life had changed irrevocably—it would never be the same.

She clenched her jaw against a sob and stepped around the side of the building. The darkness was complete there, but the past two days had given Miranda plenty of time to become familiar with the grounds. Here, where the shadows were deepest, stone benches sat in shrub-lined alcoves. She sought one out and lowered herself onto it, ignoring the cold that seeped through her jeans. The night enfolded her, the muffled sounds of traffic a backdrop to her thoughts.

She rested her elbows on her knees and lowered her head into her hands, wanting to pray, but not sure what to pray for. Peace? Acceptance? Forgiveness? The words wouldn't form, her thoughts refusing to coalesce. How could she pray when she didn't know what to ask for? And how could she know what to ask for when she couldn't even begin to imagine tomorrow, let alone a week, month or year from now? She'd spent the past ten years planning her schedule around Justin. With him gone, the future stretched out in front of her, a blank slate—empty and more frightening than she wanted to admit.

Eventually, Miranda would find a way to let go of the past and move on to the future, find a way to build a life that didn't include her nephew's special needs and unique gifts. But not tonight. Tonight she'd do nothing at all. Not plan. Not think. Not worry about the empty years stretching out in front of her.

Minutes ticked by, the soft sounds of the night filling her ears, the sweet scent of grass and leaves tickling her nose. Her arms were chilled, her body shivering with cold, but she didn't want to leave her quiet refuge. Not yet. Instead, she sat in silence, listening to the melody of night creatures mixed with the soft hum of faraway traffic.

At first the low rumble blended with all the other sounds, the rough purr no different than those of the other cars and trucks that passed by. But soon it grew louder and the noisy intrusion drew Miranda's attention.

She cocked her head, listening. The sound seemed to come from behind the building, but there was no parking lot there, just a wide expanse of grass and a gently sloping yard that led to a far-off road. Grass crunched beneath tires, the quiet rumble of the engine becoming a low roar. Then there was silence so sudden and complete Miranda's breathing sounded harsh and loud in comparison. She forced herself to take a slow, deep breath, exhaling quietly as she waited to hear more. When the silence continued, she was sure she'd been mistaken, that a car hadn't been in the backyard at all, that what she'd heard had come from another direction altogether.

A door slammed, the sound so close Miranda jumped, biting back a shriek and scrambling to her feet. Voices whispered into the darkness, the tones masculine, gruff and definitely coming from behind the building. Whatever was going on, it wasn't any of Miranda's business. The best thing she could do was head back to the front of the funeral home and leave. But something pulled her toward the back corner, some strange urging that wouldn't let her walk away. Her heart hammered against her ribs. Fast. Hard. Insistent. Telling her what she already knew—that she should be walking away from, not toward, the voices.

But it was too late. She could already make out the words, already hear what was being said.

"…crematory is a better idea."

"Takes too long. Cleaning crew will be here at midnight. We'll bring him out to the cemetery."

"It's closed. If someone sees us there and calls the cops—"

"You've got a funeral tomorrow morning, right?"

"Yeah, but—"

"So who's going to think anything of you being at the cemetery? No one. That's who. We'll just drop our friend in the newly dug grave, throw in some dirt. Tomorrow the casket goes in on top of him and, *voilà,* our problems are solved."

"I don't like it. Someone sees us out there messing around with a grave—"

"Who's going to see? The gate is locked. No one goes there after dark."

"Like I said, I don't like it. This whole business stinks like—"

"Yeah, so let's get a move on and get the key to the cemetery gate so we can get it over with."

"Fine. Sure. Get it over with. Stay here with Morran. I'll go in and get the key."

"You think I'm staying out here alone with him? No way. Now, come on. We don't have all night."

The men fell silent, their words hanging in the air, wrapping around Miranda and pulling her into something she was sure she didn't want to be part of. She needed to move away. Quietly, cautiously. Then, once she was safe, call the police.

But she couldn't. Not when she might be the only witness to a horrific crime. She crept toward the corner of the building, holding her breath, afraid the smallest sound would alert the men. Pale moonlight illuminated the backyard and an SUV parked there. Three men moved toward the funeral home, weaving a bit as they went, their shoulders pressed close together, their heads bent. They might have been college boys home from a night of partying but for the hostility that emanated from them.

And Miranda knew her fear was warranted. Knew something horrible was going on. Something violent. Something potentially deadly. Her breath hitched, her eyes straining to see more details, to take in every nuance of the picture. If she got out of this....*when* she got out of this, she wanted to have plenty to tell the police, but the rising moon shone behind the men, casting their faces into shadow. Whoever they were, whatever they planned remained hidden.

A key scraped against a lock and a door creaked open, dim light spilling out onto the faces of the men. Miranda blinked, biting back a gasp as she caught her first clear sight of them. Two she recognized. Liam Jefferson and Randy Simmons were regulars at Miranda's bakery. Both were well known in the community, one a police officer, the other the director of the funeral home. Miranda couldn't imagine either being involved in anything illegal. At least she wouldn't have been able to imagine it before tonight.

Now she had no doubt as to their true nature. Not when the third man stood between them, blindfolded, his mouth duct taped, his arms pulled tight behind his back. Was this the *friend* Liam and Randy planned to cover with dirt? She'd thought she was hearing details of a crime being hidden, a murder already committed. The truth was so much more horrible than that.

Or it would be if she didn't stop it.

No way could she run and leave the man to die. She'd wait until Liam and Randy went into the building, call the police, and then try to get close enough to read the license plate on the SUV.

As the men disappeared into the funeral home, Miranda dug through her purse, searching for her cell phone, her damp palm sliding over keys, a packet of tissue, a bottle of aspirin.

The phone wasn't there.

In her mind's eye she could see it, sitting on the kitchen counter, charging. Completely useless.

"Stupid. Stupid, stupid, stupid. Of all the nights to leave it at home." Her whispered words sounded harsh, her breath uneven. She'd write the license plate number down, then run to a neighboring house, pray someone was home and would let her use a phone.

The plan had barely formed when the door creaked open again. Randy stepped outside first, his gravely words carrying on the night air. "I don't know about this, Lee. It doesn't feel right."

Liam stepped out next, tugging the blindfolded man, then shoving him ahead a few steps while he turned to close the door. "It doesn't have to feel right. It just has to be done."

"But—"

"But nothing. Morran is scum. Getting rid of him will be doing the world a favor."

"And saving our behinds."

"Yeah, well that's the whole point, isn't it? Now get him in the car."

Randy seemed to stiffen at the harsh tone, but obeyed, reaching out for his prisoner's arm. He never had a chance to grab it. In a flash of movement the blind-folded man lashed out with a foot, knocking him to the ground.

Miranda gasped, jerked back, then froze as Liam swung toward her. His eyes probed the shadows where she stood, his gaze sweeping the corner of the building. She wanted to run, but knew any movement would have him swooping down on her. Her heart hammered double-time as she waited for discovery. But Liam turned away, stepping back toward the man who stood still as stone, giving no indication that he had moved. Miranda wanted to call out, to warn him, but thick, cottony fear trapped her words. Liam took a step closer and the man pivoted, slamming a foot into his stomach.

Now both Liam and Randy were down, but they wouldn't be for long. Already, they were struggling up. It wouldn't take much time for them to subdue their bound and blindfolded prisoner, to drag him away. To kill him.

Miranda glanced around, looking for help, for inspiration, for some way to undo what was being done. Her gaze lit on a large planter that sat near the wall of the funeral home. As weapons went, it wasn't much.

But it was all she had.

Praying for strength and for the element of surprise, Miranda moved toward it.

TWO

Hawke Morran had no intention of dying. Not tonight anyway. He had payback to deliver and he wasn't heading to the great beyond until he did so. If he hadn't been gagged, he would have told his captors as much, but Jefferson hadn't taken chances. Not only was Hawke gagged and trussed, he was blindfolded. Unfortunately for Jefferson, he hadn't killed Hawke when he'd had the chance. It was a mistake he'd soon regret.

Hawke had managed to knock both men off their feet, but the rustle of movement and huff of their breathing told him they'd soon be back up. He stood still, waiting, knowing he might have only one chance to bring them down for good.

If he failed, he'd be buried alive.

He didn't plan to fail.

Rage fueled him, muting the pain that sliced through his skull, warming muscles already demanding a fight. Jefferson's overweight buddy attacked from the left, his wheezing breath speaking of too many cigarettes and too little exercise. Hawke turned toward him, ducking low and then coming up hard, slamming his head into the man's gut and hearing with satisfaction the crack of a rib.

Agony pierced his skull, the hit he'd taken earlier allowing him no time to celebrate his victory. Nor did Jefferson allow time for Hawke to regain his balance. He came fast and quiet, but not quietly enough. Hawke spun on the balls of his feet, slashing Jefferson's knee with his foot. The pop and scream of anguish that followed did little to satisfy Hawke's rage. He wanted more. He wanted his hands free, wanted to wrap them around Jefferson's neck until the man confessed every detail of the plan to set him up.

"Watch out!" A feminine voice cut through the haze of Hawke's pain and fury, the sound so surprising he swung toward it. It was a bad move. He knew it immediately. Years of survival in a world where one wrong move meant death had taught him how swift and final the consequences of such mistakes could be.

He pivoted back toward the attack he knew was coming, the world tilting, the pain in his skull breaking into shooting flames that seared his brain. Something flew by his face, a crack and thud following so quickly he wasn't sure he'd really heard them. Then silence. Thick. Heavy. Filled with a million possibilities. None of them good.

Footsteps rustled through grass, slow, cautious. Not the full-on attack Hawke expected. The air around him shifted, the scent of apples and cinnamon wafting toward him, mellow, sweet and completely unexpected.

He tensed, waited.

Fingers brushed his arm. Gentle, trembling, hesitant. "Are you okay?"

He nodded, gritting his teeth at the stars shooting through his head.

"Okay. Wait here. I'm going to find a phone. Call the

police." The voice was breathless and shaky, the fingers that brushed against his forearm starting to slip away.

He managed to grab them, holding tight when she would have pulled away. Whoever she was, whatever she'd come here for, she'd gotten herself into a mess of trouble. Leaving and calling the police wouldn't change that.

"You want me to untie you first." It wasn't a question, but Hawke nodded anyway. He'd been determined to escape before. Now, he was desperate to. If he didn't, he wouldn't be the only one lying at the bottom of another man's grave.

The woman's fingers danced over the tape that bound his wrists, pulling gently as if she were afraid of hurting him.

Come on, lady. Hurry up. He wanted to shout the words, convey by his tone just how desperate their situation was, but the tape over his mouth kept him mute, and he was forced to stand silent while she worked. Sweat beaded his brow, the dizzying pain in his head making him nauseous, but he wouldn't give in to it. There was too much at stake.

Finally the tape loosened and he twisted his wrists, breaking through what was left of his bonds. The blindfold was next. Then the tape that covered his mouth.

He swung around, caught sight of the woman who'd freed him.

Soft. That was his first impression. Soft hair, soft full lips and soft eyes that widened as she took in his appearance. It was a reaction Hawke was used to and he ignored it, turning to search for his enemies. They were both on the ground. The heavier man lay in a heap, quiet groans issuing from between puffy lips. Jefferson was sprawled a few feet away from his buddy, a gun an arm's length away and bits of a clay pot scattered around him. "Looks like it's time to add flower pots to the list of deadly weapons."

"Deadly? I hope I didn't kill him." The woman's voice was as soft as her appearance, her hair swinging forward as she leaned toward Jefferson.

Hawke put a hand on her arm, stopping her before she could check for his pulse. "He's not dead."

But Hawke was tempted to finish him off. He might have if the woman hadn't been watching him with wide, frightened eyes, or if his own moral code hadn't altered drastically in the past year. An eye for an eye had once been his motto. Lately, that had changed. He hadn't quite figured out what it had changed to, but killing Jefferson was no longer an option.

Somewhere in the distance, a siren blared to life, the sound spurring Hawke's sluggish brain to action. "We need to get out of here."

He moved forward, grabbed the gun that lay by Jefferson, checked the safety. He could feel the woman's gaze, her fear and coiled tension.

"What are you doing?" she whispered, her voice shaky.

"Making sure we have protection."

"Protection? From what? Neither of them look like they're getting up anytime soon."

"It's not them I'm worried about."

"Then who?"

"I'll explain everything later. Right now, we need to get out of here."

"You're right. We need to call for help." She started away, moving toward the side of the building.

Hawke lunged forward, grabbing her arm. "Not yet."

She tried to pull back, but he didn't release his hold, just tugged her toward the SUV.

"Let me go." The panic in her voice might have made him hesitate if he weren't so sure hesitation would mean death.

"I can't."

"Sure you can." She jerked against his hold, her face a pale oval in the moonlight. "Just open your fingers and let me walk away."

"If you leave here without me there's a good possibility you won't live to see tomorrow. I don't want that on my conscience." He didn't give her a chance to argue, just pulled open the door of the SUV and glanced inside.

As he'd expected the keys were in the ignition. Another mistake Jefferson was going to regret making. "Get in."

"I'm not—"

"I said, *get in.*" He half lifted, half shoved her into the car.

"Hey! What are you doing?"

"Scoot over." Hawke ignored the woman's protest, sliding into the car and giving her no choice but to move into the passenger seat.

She scrambled for the door, and he snagged her shirt, holding her in place with one hand and firing up the engine with the other. Even with the windows closed, the sound of sirens was audible and growing louder. Hawke pressed down on the gas, gunning the engine and sending the SUV shooting up the slope of a hill toward a distant road. If he was lucky, he'd make it there and be able to hide the SUV in heavy Friday-night traffic. Unfortunately, he'd never had much luck.

Maybe, though, for the sake of the woman who'd saved him, God might grant him his fair share tonight.

"Stop the car! Let me out!" The passenger door flew open, and Hawke just managed to grab the woman's hand before she could jump from the vehicle.

"Do you want to get yourself killed?" His roar froze her in place. Or maybe it was the sight of the ground speeding by that kept her from pulling from his hold and leaping out.

Hawke slowed the SUV, afraid his seatbelt-less passenger would fly out on the next bounce. "Close the door."

"I'd rather you stop the car so I can get out." Her voice shook and her hand trembled violently as she tugged against his hold, but there was no mistaking her determination.

She didn't know him, didn't know the situation and probably assumed the worst. If he'd had time to explain, he would have, but he didn't. Not with death following so close behind them.

He released her hand, pulled the gun from the waistband of his jeans and pointed it toward the already terrified woman, ruthlessly shoving aside every shred of compassion he felt for her. "I said, close the door."

She hesitated and he wondered if she'd take a chance and jump. Finally, she reached for the handle and pulled the door closed, her body tense and trembling.

"Where are you taking me?"

"Somewhere safe."

"Where exactly is that?"

"I'll let you know when I figure it out." Hawke winced as the SUV bumped over a curb, its tires sliding onto smooth pavement. Traffic was lighter then he'd expected, and he merged onto the road, picking up speed and hoping that would be enough to discourage his passenger from trying to jump out again. Being distracted didn't figure into his escape plan. Then again, escaping with a woman who looked like she belonged in a cozy home with a couple of kids playing at her feet wasn't part of his plan, either.

So he'd have to make a new plan. Fast.

But first, he needed to get to a safe place.

Miranda fisted her hand around her purse and tried to control her breathing. If she hyperventilated and passed out there'd be no chance of escape. The man beside her still held the gun pointed in her direction. Though his gaze was fixed on the road, Miranda was sure he was aware of every move she made. A few minutes ago he'd seemed a helpless victim who needed saving. Now she wasn't so sure.

Something flashed in the periphery of her vision, and she glanced in the side mirror, catching sight of blue and white lights in the distance. Hope made her heart leap and her pulse race.

Please let them be coming for us.

But even as she mumbled the prayer, her dark-haired kidnapper took the beltway ramp, speeding into traffic with barely a glance at oncoming vehicles. Miranda gasped, releasing her purse so that she could hold on to the seat. The lights had disappeared from view, but the car's speed and swift lane changes should attract more police attention.

If it didn't get Miranda and her kidnapper killed first.

As if he sensed her thoughts, the man eased up on the gas and pulled into the slow lane, dashing Miranda's hope of rescue. Tense with worry, sick with dread, she prayed desperately for some way out, her gaze scanning the cars that passed, her mind scrambling for a plan. Any plan.

"If you let me out here, I won't press charges."

"Charges?"

"Kidnapping is a serious crime."

"Kidnapping? Is that what you call this?"

"What would you call it?"

"Returning a favor. You saved my life. Now I'm doing the same for you." His voice was harsh, an exotic accent adding depth and richness to the words, but doing nothing to soften the tone.

"It's hard to believe that's what you're doing when you're pointing a gun at me."

"Sorry. It seemed the only way to keep you from doing something we'd both regret." He tucked the gun back into the waistband of his jeans, his movements economical and practiced, as if he'd done the same a thousand times before.

And somehow, looking at his chiseled face and the scar that bisected it from cheekbone to chin, Miranda had a feeling he had. She slid closer to the door, wishing they were in bumper-to-bumper traffic or that she dared jump out of a car traveling sixty miles an hour. But they weren't, she didn't. She was reduced to sitting terrified as she was driven farther and farther from home.

She eyed the man, the door, the traffic speeding by. Maybe she could attract someone's attention with a gesture or an expression. Maybe—

"Whatever you're thinking, forget it." He wasn't even looking her way, yet seemed to sense her intentions.

She stiffened, turning to face him again. "I'm not thinking anything."

"Sure you are. You're thinking about opening the door and jumping for it. Or maybe attracting someone's attention." He shrugged. "It's what I'd do if I were in your position."

"And if I were in *your* position, I'd stop the car and let my prisoner out." She tried to put confidence in her voice, tried to sound less scared than she felt.

"You're not a prisoner."

"Then what am I?"

"The newest member of the witness protection program."

Miranda blinked, not sure she'd heard right. "Are you with the FBI?"

He hesitated and Miranda had the feeling he was trying to decide how much of the truth to tell her. When he finally answered, his tone was much more gentle than it had been before. "No, but I plan to be just as effective in keeping you safe."

"I don't need you to keep me safe. I need you to let me go."

"Then it would have been better if you'd walked away and left me to deal with Jefferson on my own."

"He was trying to kill you."

"And now he's going to try to kill us both." His tone was grim, his jaw tight, and Miranda had no doubt he believed what he was saying.

She just wasn't sure she did. "Why?"

"Because I'm a threat and because you were in the wrong place at the wrong time and were foolish enough to let him know it."

"What else was I suppose to do? Let him kill you?"

"Let whatever was to happen, happen."

"I couldn't."

"Then maybe you'll understand why I can't let you go." His tone was softer than Miranda would have expected from such a hard-looking man and she studied his profile, wishing she could read more in his face.

"Who are you?" The question popped out, though Miranda wasn't sure what answer she hoped for—a name, an occupation, some clue as to who she was dealing with.

"Hawke Morran." He answered the question without actually answering it. The name doing nothing to explain who Hawke was or why Liam had been trying to kill him.

"Who are you to Liam?"

"Liam? You know Jefferson?" The gentleness was gone, replaced by a harshness that made Miranda cringe.

"Everyone in Essex knows him."

"I'm not interested in everyone. I'm interested in you. You say you know him. Does *he* know *you?* Your name? Where you live?"

Did he? Miranda was sure he knew her name, and there was no doubt he knew where she worked, he visited the bakery several times a week. It would be easy enough to get her address. "Probably."

Hawke muttered something in a language Miranda didn't recognize, the words unintelligible, the frustration behind them obvious.

Her own frustration rose, joining the fear that pounded frantically through her blood. She'd done what she thought was right. Now, she'd pay for it. That seemed to be a pattern in her life. "I own a business in

Essex. Lots of people know me. Liam just happens to be one of them."

"He also just happens to be a murderer."

Miranda didn't need the reminder. She'd seen Liam in action; watched him pull a gun on a bound and blind-folded man, had seen the cold determination in his eyes as he'd caught sight of her. She had known then that she was seconds from death. "We need to go to the police and tell them what happened before Liam hurts someone else."

"No."

"What do you mean, no?"

"Exactly what I said. I've got a phony criminal record. The police won't believe anything I have to say. You're with me. It stands to reason they won't believe you, either." He glanced her way, his gaze searing into hers before he turned his attention back to the road.

"Why—"

"We'll discuss it all later." His tone was curt and dis-missive, the kind that brooked no argument.

And Miranda didn't want to argue. She wanted to let things play out the way they would. Just as she had so many times before. With her sister. Her mother. Her father. Boyfriends. It always seemed so much easier to go with the flow than to fight against the tide. This time, though, the tide was dragging her out into dan-gerous waters and she had a feeling that if she didn't fight it she'd be pulled under. "Later isn't good enough. I want answers now."

He shrugged, but didn't speak as he steered the SUV onto an off-ramp.

The neighborhood he drove through was battered, the houses 1970s cookie cutters, every street lined with pickup trucks and scrap-metal cars. Miranda knew the area—a tough, crime-ridden neighborhood on the edge of D.C. When Hawke pulled into a driveway, she put her hand on the door, ready to yank it open and flee, but he grabbed her arm, his hand a steel band trapping her in place.

His breath fanned her cheek as he leaned close. "We're getting out my side, walking around to the back of the house, getting a new ride and you're not going to do anything foolish. Time isn't on our side and I don't want to waste any of it chasing after you. All right?"

The memory of the gun he'd tucked into his waistband spurred Miranda to do as he said, her heart pounding a sickening beat as Hawke tugged her across the front seat and out the door.

The moon shone bright and yellow in the navy sky and the crisp air chilled Miranda's clammy skin as Hawke hurried her around the side of a house.

An old garage stood at the back of the property and he punched numbers into a security pad on the door, then tugged Miranda to a dark sedan inside.

"Get in." His words were gruff, his hand gentle as he pressed it against her shoulder, urging her to do as he'd commanded.

The car door slammed with a finality that stilled the breath in Miranda's lungs. She shouldn't be allowing this. Crime prevention experts said it all the time—never get in a car with your attacker. Never let him take you away from the scene.

And here she was, doing exactly that.

But Hawke wasn't an attacker. He was a man who'd almost been killed. A man she'd saved. Now he claimed to be saving her. She wasn't sure if she believed him.

All she knew was that eventually there'd be a chance to escape. She could only pray that when it came, she'd know for sure whether or not she should take it.

THREE

Hawke's head throbbed with every movement, every sound reverberating through his brain. He ignored the pain, determined to put as much distance between his new ride and the SUV as possible. It wasn't just his life on the line this time. He had his passenger to worry about, as well.

Who was she? What had brought her to the funeral home so late at night? Not the hope of scoring drugs. Hawke was almost sure of that, though he'd been sure of things before and been proven wrong.

He risked a quick glance in her direction, gritting his teeth at the renewed throbbing in his head. The woman's arms were crossed at her waist, her eyes trained straight ahead. She looked scared, not high on drugs. "What's your name?"

His words must have startled her. She jerked, her arm brushing against his side, her breath leaving on a quick, raspy gasp. "Miranda. Sheldon."

"Miranda." The name rolled off his tongue as if he'd said it a thousand times before. "What were you doing at a funeral home so late at night?"

"I was taking a walk." There was more to it than that.

Hawke was sure of it, though he couldn't blame her for denying him answers.

"And while you were walking you saved my life."

"Would you rather I had walked away and let you die?"

"Other people would have."

"I'm not other people. I'm me."

"And who is that, Miranda Sheldon? Besides a woman caught up in something she didn't ask for?"

"Just your everyday, average American." Her words were quiet, barely audible above the rumbling of the car and the slushing agony in his skull, but Hawke heard.

He glanced at Miranda again. The softness he'd noticed when he'd first seen her was only magnified in the close confines of the car. Smooth skin. Shiny hair that fell to her shoulders. Lips and face unadorned. Short unpainted nails. No rings. No jewelry of any kind. Apples. Cinnamon. A sweetness that was obvious even while she was afraid for her life. "There is nothing average or everyday about a woman who'd risk her own life for someone else."

She didn't respond and he knew he should be glad. He needed to plan his next move, not carry on a conversation. He rubbed the back of his neck, ignoring the blood that seeped from his head and coated his fingers. To formulate a plan he'd need more information and he knew just where to get it.

He yanked open the glove compartment and pulled out the cell phone he kept there, pushing speed dial to connect with the one number stored on it. The phone rang once before it was picked up.

"Stone, here." Noah Stone's voice was tight and gruff, and Hawke knew that the call had been expected.

A former DEA agent, Noah was one of the few people who knew Hawke was in the States and what he was doing there. Of those privy to Hawke's mission, Noah was the only one he trusted.

"It's Hawke."

"I thought you might be calling."

"So you've already heard?"

"That you murdered the agent you were working with and stole fifty thousand dollars cash? Who hasn't?"

"I didn't steal fifty thousand dollars."

"That leaves the question of murder open."

"Smithfield was dead when I got to the rendezvous." Lying in a pool of his own blood, his head split open.

"Murdered with a machete that had your fingerprints all over it."

"It should. It's mine. I left it in Thailand nine months ago." And yet it was here. He'd seen it with his own eyes—the flat blade and carved-bone handle worn from years of use in the jungles of Mae Hong Son. He'd been leaning down to examine it when he'd been hit from behind.

Which could only mean one thing. Someone in Thailand had set this up, had probably been planning it from the day the DEA had called Hawke in and offered him a job.

Hot anger speared through him, frustration making him want to hurl the phone out the car's window. He tightened his hand around it and growled into the phone. "Look, Stone, if you don't believe that I'm innocent we've got nothing more to say to each other."

"I'm on your side in this, Hawke, but I'm standing alone. Whoever set you up did it perfectly. The fingerprints on the weapon have every cop in the contiguous United States looking for you."

"What about the DEA?"

Noah's hesitation spoke volumes. The Drug Enforcement Agency might have hired Hawke to bring down one of the most notorious drug dealers on the East Coast, but they didn't trust him.

"So, they think I'm guilty."

"They're reserving judgment."

"Until?"

"Until they talk to you and your accomplice."

Hawke gritted his teeth, shot a look at Miranda. She was eyeing the phone as if a knight in shining armor might be on the other end of the line, ready to ride to her rescue. Unfortunately, Hawke was the only one riding anywhere and he was no knight. "Accomplice? You going to tell me who that is?"

"A woman. Apparently, the two of you have been seeing each other for several months. According to your coworkers at Green's factory, you spent more time with her than with anyone else."

"Green works fast."

"If he didn't, he would have been out of business and in jail years ago."

It was true. One of the East Coast's most successful drug traffickers, Harold Green was, by most people's accounts, an upstanding citizen of Essex, Maryland. A churchgoer, city council member and business owner, he hid his true nature beneath a facade of respectability. The DEA had hired Hawke to infiltrate Green's organization and to bring him down. He'd have succeeded if he hadn't been betrayed.

Fury threatened to take hold, but he tamped it down.

Losing control meant losing. And Hawke had no intention of doing that. "What else?"

"Word is, you were apprehended by a Maryland cop. Your accomplice took him by surprise, knocking him out, and you both escaped."

"Any news of a second man involved in that?"

"No. Just Liam Jefferson. Why? Was someone else there?"

"Yeah. The director of one of Green's funeral homes. Simmons. Randy."

"Do you think we should be looking for another body?"

"Yeah, but I don't think you'll find one. Green is nothing if not thorough. He won't leave any loose ends."

"Including you."

"Including me." Or Miranda, but Hawke didn't add the thought.

There was another moment of hesitation. "You know you need to turn yourself in."

"Do I?"

"What other option do you have?"

"I can get back home, find out who set me up and get the evidence I need to prove it."

"I take it you have an idea how this should be done?"

"You've got connections on both sides of the law. If I can make it down to your area, can you get me out of the country?"

"I've got some people that owe me favors. I'll call them in. See what I can do."

Hawke had hoped Noah would agree, but hadn't been certain. Relief loosened his grip on the phone, eased some of the pounding pain in his head. "How long will it take?"

"Give me an hour."

"Thanks."

"We're friends. I trust you. Just don't let your need for revenge keep you from doing what's right."

"You're telling me not to kill the person who set me up." A few years ago, he might have. Hawke had changed since then. Stone was part of the reason for that, though Hawke doubted he knew it.

"Taking the law into your hands won't solve anything, and it'll only make more trouble for you."

"This isn't just about me anymore, Stone." He glanced at Miranda, saw that she was watching with wide, dark eyes. "You've been pulled into it. So has the woman who's with me. I won't risk either of you for revenge. I give you my word on that."

"One hour, then." Noah disconnected and Hawke tossed the phone into Miranda's lap.

Now that he had the means to get her out of harms way, he'd make sure she had reason to cooperate. Flying halfway around the world with someone determined to escape was low on Hawke's lists of ways to keep from being noticed.

She stared down at the phone, but didn't reach for it, her hands fisted at her side, her jaw set.

"Is there someone you want to call? Someone who might be worried?

"Yes."

"Then call." And if news was spreading as fast as Noah claimed, Miranda would hear just how much trouble she was in from someone she trusted.

Call? Miranda was sure Hawke would pull the phone from her hands as she lifted it, but he looked relaxed. Much more relaxed than he'd been before his phone call. He'd mentioned leaving the country. Maybe he planned to drop her off and let her return home. Miranda refused to contemplate anything else. She dialed, pressing the phone to her ear, her heart thrumming a frantic beat. Please, Lauren, pick up. For once be there for me.

"Hello?" Lauren's voice filled the line, high-pitched and breathless.

"Lauren, it's me. I—"

"Miranda! Thank goodness! Where are you?"

Miranda glanced at a road sign, almost gave her sister the exit number, but hesitated. There was an edge of hysteria in Lauren's voice, a breathless quality to it that didn't fit. It wasn't like her to be overly concerned with anyone but herself. That she was so upset could only mean bad news. "What's wrong, Lauren?"

"Wrong? You attack a police officer and you're asking me what's wrong?"

Miranda went cold at her words, her back rigid with mounting tension. "How did you hear about that?"

"How do you think I heard about it? The police are here. They don't take kindly to having one of their own knocked unconscious."

"I didn't have a choice. Liam—"

"Don't say anything else, sis." Her brother Max cut in, his voice such a welcome relief Miranda's eyes burned with threatening tears.

"Max. I thought your plane wasn't coming in until the morning."

"I took an earlier flight. It's a good thing I did. You're in a lot of trouble, kid."

"I didn't do anything wrong, Max. This is all some kind of misunderstanding. I—"

"We'll talk when you get home. The line is being monitored by the police. I don't want you to say anything else until we're face to face."

"I don't have anything to hide." But her palms were sweaty, her breath hitching with fear.

"You need to come home, Randa. Max and I are here for you. We'll support you. No matter what. Max has found you a great lawyer. The best. I've already paid a retainer fee. It's the least I could do." Lauren's words caught on a sob. "After all, this is my fault. The past few years…all your time spent caring for Justin. I should have known you needed more than that."

"Your fault? What are you talking about? I went for a walk and—"

"Don't say anything." Max nearly shouted the words, his panic scaring Miranda more than all Lauren's sobs could. Older than her by fifteen years, Max had been more father than brother to Miranda, a calm steadying influence in a chaotic, unstable home.

"Tell me what's happening. Tell me what you think I did." Miranda's panic rose with Max's.

"*I* don't think you did anything. It's the police who are accusing you." Max bit out the words, his anger preferable to panic. "According to them, you've been dating a felon. The two of you plotted to steal fifty-thousand dollars from a DEA agent. The agent was found dead an hour ago."

Miranda's gaze leaped to Hawke. He'd said nothing about a murdered DEA agent. But then, he hadn't said much about anything.

"Miranda? Are you still there?" Max's words pulled her from her thoughts and she took a deep breath, trying to force a calm to her voice that she didn't feel.

"I'm here. I haven't been dating anyone, haven't stolen anything. I haven't done anything wrong. I've got plenty of friends who will verify that. All my time has been spent with Justin. You know that."

"It isn't about what I know or what I believe or even what you tell me is going on. It's about proof. And right now the police have witnesses willing to testify that they saw you and their suspect together on more than one occasion."

"What witnesses? What are you talking about?"

"Coworkers and friends. Add to that Sergeant Jefferson's testimony—"

Miranda stiffened, her muscles so taut she thought they might shatter. "About what?"

"About seeing you and the suspect together at your bakery."

"That's a lie!"

"Yeah? Well right now, it's his word against yours. He's a police officer and here. You're on the run with some guy who's got a record a mile long. Who do you think seems more believable?"

"Max—"

"Tell me where you are, Miranda. I'll come get you and we'll work things out. I promise." His tone was persuasive, the same one he'd used so often to try to convince Lauren to do the right thing. He'd never had to convince Miranda.

Even now, she wanted to respond, to tell him what he wanted to hear, but the words died on her tongue, her mind shouting a warning that she couldn't ignore. Liam had already told his side of the story. The police believed him, Miranda's family seemed to believe him and, as much as *she'd* like to believe that people would step forward to defend her, Miranda knew the truth was much more grim. Her friends knew too little about her life to say with any certainty how she spent her days. Taking care of Justin had required most of her time and energy. She'd had little of either left for friendship. If she returned home now, she'd be arrested.

Or worse.

And if that happened, Max would go after whoever had hurt her.

An image of Liam pointing a gun at Hawke flashed through her mind and she imagined Max on the other end of the barrel, imagined the loud crack of gunfire and her brother falling lifeless to the ground. She couldn't risk it, couldn't allow him to be pulled into danger with her.

"Miranda? Are you still there?"

"I'm here, but I can't come home yet, Max. Not until I can prove that I'm innocent."

"We'll find the proof together." The pain in his voice was palpable, stretching across the phone line and wrapping around her heart.

"I love you, Max. Thanks for being such a great big brother."

With that she hung up the phone, her pulse pounding, her mind racing, the truth of what she'd just done a hard, cold knot in her stomach. She'd cut her ties with home, turned her back on Max and put her life in the hands of a man she didn't know and wasn't sure she trusted. She could only pray she hadn't made a terrible mistake, because she was sure there would be no turning back. Only moving forward into the terrifying unknown.

FOUR

"**D**id the phone call not go the way you wanted?" Hawke broke into Miranda's thoughts, his voice gravely and harsh.

"You knew it wouldn't."

"I knew that it would give you a truth you might not have accepted from me."

"What truth? That I'm wanted for accessory to murder?"

"That returning home isn't the answer to your troubles."

"And staying with you is?"

"It's better than the alternative."

"Which is?"

"Your body rotting in a shallow grave somewhere."

"You act like it's a done deal."

"Walk away from me and it is. Stay with me and we'll find what we need to prove our innocence. Once Liam and Green are behind bars, you can safely return to your family."

What family?

As much as Miranda loved Max, he had a life completely separate from hers, his Chicago apartment too small to offer guest quarters, his accounting firm busy enough to make vacationing nearly impossible. Lauren was the opposite, traveling the world as a runway model and only stopping to visit Justin when she couldn't put it off any longer. Or that's what she'd done before. Now that her son was gone, Lauren would probably never return to Maryland. Which meant Miranda would be returning to an empty house, a business and memories.

She shoved the thought aside, forcing back the sorrow that came with it. "How long will it take?"

"I don't know."

"I need to be home tomorrow." For Justin's funeral. She didn't add the last, knowing the words would mean nothing to the cold-eyed man beside her.

"Sorry, babe. That's not going to happen."

She'd known it, but she'd hoped anyway, the small part of herself that refused to believe that things were as bad as they seemed telling her that everything would be okay in the morning. A few more hours of darkness and she'd wake from the nightmare. Wasn't that what she'd told herself when she'd been a kid, the darkness pressing in around her, filled with monsters? "Then what? A few days? A week? I've got a business to run. I can't be away from it for long."

"Will your business matter if you're dead?"

There was nothing to say to that, so she remained silent, turning away from Hawke and staring out the car window.

Outside, life continued as always, people traveling home from restaurants, friends and parties, making plans for the next day as they ended this one. A week ago, Miranda had been doing the same, leaving home on Friday evening to attend a bridal shower on the eastern shore. With Lauren committed to caring for Justin until the following night, Miranda had imagined hours spent window shopping, sampling pastries from local bakeries, enjoying the simple pleasure of no responsibility for the first time in way too many months.

And in one moment of senseless tragedy it had all changed.

Even if she made it home in one piece, life would never be what it had once been. Hot tears filled Miranda's eyes, but she forced them away. Crying couldn't bring her nephew back. Nor would it change her situation. Only God could do that, and she wasn't sure He would. Watching Justin die while she prayed for him to be healed had been the hardest thing she'd ever done. In the dark hours after his death, she'd wondered if God heard her frantic pleading or if He even cared. Now, she wanted desperately to grasp her tattered faith, to believe that He would work everything out for the best.

"You're crying." The gritty texture of Hawke's voice matched the rough callus on the finger he swept down her cheek.

Her skin heated in the wake of his touch and she brushed her hand down the same path his finger had traced, wiping away tears she hadn't realized she was shedding. "No, I'm not."

"I suppose the moisture on your cheeks is nothing."

"A few tears on my cheeks doesn't mean I'm crying."

"No? Then what does it mean?"

"That I'm releasing some pent-up emotion."

Hawke chuckled, a deep rumble that was a soothing balm against her frazzled nerves. "You're an interesting lady, Miranda."

Interesting? *Quiet, sweet, helpful,* those were the words most often used to describe her. Never interesting.

Before she had a chance to respond, Hawke's cell phone rang and he lifted it to his ear.

"What's up?" The words were his only greeting, his scowl deepening as the caller spoke. "What time? We'll be there." He dropped the phone onto the console, pulled the car onto a side road, then another and another until Miranda wasn't sure where they were or which direction they were headed. Finally, he pulled into the parking lot of a convenience store and turned to face her.

"We've got a decision to make."

"We?" He acted as if they were a team, working together toward a common goal. And maybe they were, but it didn't feel that way. Not when Hawke knew so much more about what was going on then she did. And not when he seemed so determined to keep it that way.

"We." He winced, putting a hand up to the back of his head and bringing it down again, something shiny and moist staining his fingers.

"You're bleeding." Miranda reached out, wanting to help, but Hawke's quick, hard glance froze her in place.

"I'll live." His hand fisted around the steering wheel, his knuckles white. "We have more important things to worry about. We've got six hours to make it to Lakeview, Virginia. Do you know it?"

"No."

He nodded. "We'll map it out in a minute. My friend will have transportation waiting for us there. If we're late, we may not have a second chance."

"A second chance at what?"

"Someone set me up, Miranda. Planned everything that happened tonight to make me look guilty of a crime I didn't commit. Do you believe that?"

"I don't know what I believe."

"You're honest, at least."

"And you haven't answered my question. What won't we have a second chance at?"

"Getting out of the state. Out of the country."

"Out of the country?" She tried out the words, found them bitter on her tongue. "No."

"If we stay here, we'll be caught. I've got few friends that I can turn to. No one that I'm willing to drag into this mess. My home is in Thailand. The DEA recruited me there. They hired me to come to the States and bring down a drug trafficker named Green."

"Harold Green?" He owned several businesses in Essex. A moving company, a local grocery store. The funeral home.

"Right. He's been importing drugs from Thailand for years, selling them, then laundering the money through his businesses. The DEA knows it, but finding the proof to close him down and put him away has been difficult."

"So they sent you to do it for them?"

"I was sent in deep under cover. The only people who know I'm working the case are in Thailand. Their hope is that once they pull Green in, he'll give them the names of his overseas contacts. I think someone in Thailand doesn't want that to happen. Someone working for the DEA. I plan to find out who it is. It's the only way to clear my name. And yours."

"The DEA here…"

"Thinks I murdered one of their agents."

"But—"

"Babe, we're out of time. It takes five hours to get to Lakeview. Before we get there I need to know you're with me on this."

Was she? Miranda wasn't sure she trusted her own judgement in the matter. The stakes were too high. She was too scared. "Do I have a choice?"

"I haven't decided yet." He grimaced, his jaw tight. "You saved my life. I don't want to leave you here to die because of it."

There was truth in his words, in the grim determination in his eyes as they met hers. And despite herself, despite her doubt, Miranda knew she had to go with him. If there was a way out of this, it lay in the direction Hawke was going. That, at least, she felt sure of. "I guess I'm with you on it, then."

Hawke smiled, the expression softening his face, changing it from danger to safety, from ice to warmth. "That's what I was hoping you'd say."

"So, now what?"

"Now, we head for Lakeview." He turned toward the backseat, swayed, then slumped toward Miranda, his weight pushing her back toward the door and stealing her breath.

"Hawke? Hawke!" She pushed at his chest, her heart pounding. She slid her hand up to his neck, feeling for his pulse and finding the slick warmth of blood there.

"Hawke!" She shouted in his ear, desperate for a response.

This time he groaned, shifting slightly, his chin brushing against her cheek, razor stubble scratching at her skin. She shivered, pushing at him again and finally managing to maneuver him into his seat. His head slumped forward and she could see blood pooling in the hollow of his throat.

Miranda brushed a hand against his forehead and cheek, feeling for a fever the same way she had so many times when Justin was sick. But Hawke wasn't a boy, he was a man, and he wasn't sick, he was hurt.

And Miranda had no idea how to help him.

Yes, you do. You've taken first-aid classes. You know what to do. Stop panicking and think. Check respiration and pulse. Find the wound. Stop the bleeding. Get him to a doctor.

A doctor! That's exactly what they needed. She could call 911, get an ambulance to take Hawke to the hospital while she spoke to the police and told them Hawke's story and her own. The plan seemed reasonable, good even. Except for a few small things—Hawke was wanted for murder, she was wanted as an accessory and at least one person wanted them both dead.

Miranda frowned and leaned over the seat, searching for something to staunch the flow of blood that seemed to be coming from the back of Hawke's head. She found a backpack on the floor, a map on the seat. She grabbed both, opening the first and pulling out packets of dried food, a bottle of water, a T-shirt and hat. At the bottom of the bag, she found a small plastic container. She opened it quickly, her hands shaking with adrenaline and fear. Gauze, bandages, needle, thread, several white pills packed in plastic bags, antiseptic wipes, an EpiPen—Hawke had prepared for minor medical emergencies. The only problem was, Miranda wasn't sure minor was what she was dealing with.

She pulled out the gauze, then shifted Hawke's head

to the side, trying to find the wound. Her fingers probed the flesh behind his ear, wound through silky strands of hair. At the back of his head, close to the base of his skull, a hard lump oozed warm, sticky blood. She pressed the gauze to it, wincing in sympathy, though he seemed completely unaware of her ministrations. That couldn't be good.

"Hawke?" He didn't answer, and Miranda shook his shoulder, praying for some reaction.

His eyes remained closed, his head a leaden weight against her hand.

"Now what?" She whispered the question out loud, her mind scrambling for a plan, her eyes scanning the interior of the car. Hawke's cell phone lay on the console between them, and she grabbed it. Maybe she could find the number of the person they were supposed to meet in Virginia.

She scrolled through the options, searching for an outgoing call log, praying that she'd find what she was looking for.

"What are you doing?" The words were a harsh growl, the hand that wrapped around her wrist just short of painful.

She gasped, her heart skipping a beat as she met Hawke's cold gaze. "Trying to decide if I should call for help."

He stared at her, his gaze never wavering as he straightened in his seat, slid his free hand over the gauze Miranda still held, and nudged her hand away from it. "It wouldn't have been a good idea."

His tone matched his gaze—icy and unyielding, and Miranda knew he wasn't a man who would take betrayal lightly; that he'd demand his own justice for any wrong done to him. She swallowed back her fear, tugging at the fingers still wrapped around her wrist. "You were unconscious and unresponsive. You need a doctor."

"I need to catch our ride. I need to find the man who betrayed me. I do *not* need a doctor." Hawke tried to add emphasis to his words, but they came out weaker than he intended. The fact was, he probably did need a doctor, but he didn't have time for one. *They* didn't have time for one.

"You're bleeding pretty badly." Miranda leaned in close, the scent of apples and cinnamon enveloping him.

No woman had a right to smell that good.

And Hawke had no business noticing.

Unless he missed his guess, Miranda was one of those rare people who remained untarnished by the world. He, on the other hand, was more tarnished than most.

He scowled, frustrated as much by the direction of his thoughts as he was by his physical weakness. "Bleeding is a whole lot better than being dead. Which is exactly what we'd both be if you'd been foolish enough to call an ambulance."

At his harsh words, Miranda jerked back, her face pale in the dim light, her dark hair a mass of curls around her face. Hawke knew enough about fear to recognize it in her eyes. Guilt at putting it there made him want to wrap an arm around her shoulders and reassure her that everything was going to be okay.

Instead, he kept the gauze pressed to his head with one hand and grabbed the road map with the other. "Our six hours are ticking away while we sit here arguing. Put your seat belt back on and let's go."

The fear he'd seen in Miranda's eyes disappeared, replaced by stony resolve. "I may not be able to make you see a doctor, but I'm not going to let you drive. Not when you could pass out again."

She had a point, even if Hawke didn't want to admit it. His head throbbed with each heartbeat and sudden movements made him dizzy. Losing consciousness again was a real possibility no matter how hard he might fight against it. Passing out while driving could get them both killed. Then again, giving Miranda control of the car might do the same. It would be easy enough for her to drive to a police station and turn them both in. "I've driven under worse conditions."

"And tonight you don't have to. I don't see a problem. Unless you don't trust me." She was issuing a challenge, but Hawke wasn't in the mood to meet it.

"I don't trust anyone."

"That makes two of us." She opened the car door, got out. "So, I guess we'll just have to figure out how to accomplish our goals anyway."

Hawke figured he had a few options—tell her to get out and go it alone, or pull out the gun and demand she get back into the passenger seat or let her have her way.

The first appealed only in as much as he could convince himself he didn't care if Miranda lived or died. Which wasn't much. The second might have worked, but imagining the fear and horror on her face when he pointed the gun at her made Hawke hesitate, a strange and alarming development in an already frustrating night.

"I don't like losing." He ground the words out, but Miranda just smiled.

"I guess that's another thing we have in common."

With that, she shut the door and started around the side of the car, leaving Hawke wondering how a woman who didn't look capable of hurting a fly had bested him.

FIVE

Miranda's heart slammed in her chest as she rounded the car, Hawke's words echoing in her head. The anger on his face told her just how much he didn't like losing. Yet, here she was heading around the side of the car with every intention of doing things her way. What was she thinking? He had a gun for crying out loud.

But if he planned on using it, he already would have.

Maybe she should make a break for it, run into the convenience store and ask for help. She doubted Hawke would try to stop her. Unfortunately, the same instincts that told Miranda that Hawke wouldn't hurt her, told her that she was better off with him than without. She needed answers before she could return home. Without them, she risked putting her brother and sister in harm's way—and staying with Hawke seemed the only sure way to get those answers.

She pulled open the car door, saw that Hawke had moved into the passenger seat, and did her best to act confident and unperturbed. "Where to?"

"I'll mark the route on the map. Then we'll drive straight there. No stops for anything. We've already lost enough time. We can't afford to waste any more."

He met her gaze, his expression unreadable, his anger concealed as he opened the glove compartment and pulled out a pack of highlighters.

"All right. Let's do it."

It took less than a minute for Hawke to highlight a yellow path from their location to a small town near a lake. When he finished, he highlighted a second route in blue. "The yellow route is the quickest. The blue uses the most back roads. We'll try yellow first. If there's too much police traffic, we'll switch to blue."

"Okay." Miranda's hands were moist against the steering wheel, the reality of what she was about to do pulsing through her veins. Until now, she'd felt more like a victim than an active participant in Hawke's escape, but she could no longer deny the role she was taking. Running from the police, aiding an accused killer.

If they were caught…

"You're doing this because you have to, Miranda Sheldon." Hawke's voice broke into her thoughts; his words offering assurance before she'd even voiced her doubts.

"Do I?" She whispered the question, not expecting an answer.

"If you don't, we'll both die."

"That's a worse-case scenario."

"If you really believed that, you would have run into the store and called for help instead of getting back into the car with me."

"I need answers so that I can go home. It's the only way to make sure my family is safe."

"You'll get the answers you need. *We'll* get them. And once we do, you'll have no worries about those you love." He rubbed at the back of his head, his hand coming away bloody again.

"You need to keep applying pressure to that."

"I *need* to get to Lakeview."

Miranda took the hint and started the engine, pulling out of the parking lot, following Hawke's directions back to the highway. It was late, traffic sparse, what few cars there were passing in flashes of light. Miranda should have been lulled by the darkness that stretched out before them, by the quiet hum of the car engine and by Hawke's silence.

Instead, she felt wired, her body trembling with adrenaline, everything in her begging for action. Finally, she could stand the quiet no longer. "What exactly is going to happen when we get to Lakeview? Are we taking another car? A train? A plane?"

"It would be difficult to take a train or car to Thailand." His words were so matter-of-fact they almost didn't register.

When they did, Miranda cast a quick glance in Hawke's direction, saw that he was watching her with a dark, intense gaze.

"You don't mean Thailand as in the country?"

"Do you know of another Thailand?"

"No, but I'm hoping there is one, because there is no way in the world I can go to Southeast Asia."

"Sure you can. Everything is taken care of. We'll have a passport and paperwork waiting for you."

"That's great, but I won't be needing them. I can't go. When you said out of the country I was thinking Mexico or Canada, not halfway around the world." Miranda's hands were shaking on the wheel.

"I told you that the person who betrayed me to Green

has to be in Thailand. No one here knew who I was or what I was doing."

"There must be people in Thailand who can investigate."

"I also told you, I don't trust anyone."

"You go, then. I'll stay in Lakeview."

"And what? The police know who you are. They've already issued an APB. It's only a matter of time before they find you."

"I thought....." She shook her head, knowing that she *hadn't* thought. If she had, she would have known exactly what Hawke meant when he talked about leaving the country.

"What did you think?" His words were quiet, his tone more kind than Miranda expected.

"Nothing. I guess I just hoped this would all be over by tomorrow."

"There's no way that's going to happen, babe. We've got real trouble and real trouble takes time to resolve." There was sympathy in his voice, the first he'd shown her, and Miranda's throat tightened in response.

She swallowed back tears and tried to keep her voice even. "My nephew's funeral is tomorrow. I need to be there. My sister is counting on it."

"I'm sorry for your loss. Sorry you can't be there for your sister." He shifted beside her, his palm sliding against her cheek, capturing a tear she hadn't known was falling. "But allowing yourself to get arrested will only cause your family more sorrow."

"I know." She refused to let more tears fall, refused to allow herself to lean into Hawke's touch. He was a stranger, after all. A stranger who had more hardness in him than sympathy.

"Is your nephew the reason you were at the funeral home tonight?"

"It seems silly now." She stared out the windshield, the dark night and nearly empty road stretching out before her.

"Why?"

"It's not like Justin needed me there. I just…didn't want to let him go."

"You were close?"

"I've raised him since he was two." He'd been a son to her, though saying as much would have made her feel disloyal to her sister.

"His parents are dead?"

"No. I'm not sure who his father was. My sister is a model. She traveled too much to be his caregiver."

"Your sister is a model?" He tensed, and Miranda felt her own muscles tighten.

"Yes. Why?"

"Someone the general public is familiar with?"

"She's not a supermodel, if that's what you mean, but she's been on her fair share of magazine covers. She also does runway modeling."

"So, not only do the police know who you are, but the world knows your sister. This isn't good, babe."

"The world knows Lauren, but they don't know I'm her sister." Lauren had never allowed the press any information regarding her son. In that way at least, she'd done what was best for Justin.

"It won't take long for the press to find out. Once it does, your name and face will be plastered on every news station and newspaper in the country."

"Maybe the local news, but I doubt what's happened will be of much interest anywhere else." But even as she said it, Miranda had the sinking feeling Hawke was right, that the double tragedy of losing a son and then having a sister turn felon would be enough to make Lauren headline news.

"I think you know you're wrong."

Miranda nodded, wishing she could believe otherwise. "At least Lauren doesn't have any recent pictures of me."

"Someone else will. The press always finds a way."

"They'll be hard-pressed to find anything that doesn't show me thirty pounds heavier and ten years younger." In the years since she'd been caring for Justin, Miranda had had little time to spend in activities that might have involved picture taking. Except for the occasional bridal or baby shower, the past few years had been spent at her bakery, at home or at church.

"Heavier. Younger. It won't matter. Your face is one people will notice and remember."

"I'm not that memorable."

"No?"

"No." Miranda could feel Hawke's gaze as she maneuvered the car around a slow-moving vehicle, and her cheeks heated.

"Perhaps you just don't know what people find memorable."

"And you do?"

"I've made it my business to know people." The words seemed almost a threat and Miranda wondered exactly how he used the knowledge he possessed.

"That makes one of us anyway."

"You know enough about people to stick with me. That's a start."

"I just hope I'm not making a mistake." The words

slipped out and Miranda regretted them immediately. Letting Hawke know how scared she really was, letting him see how unsure she felt, could only be a mistake. And she'd made enough of those for one night. "What I mean is—"

"Exactly what you said. Don't worry, sticking with me isn't a mistake. Whether or not you'll regret it, I can't say." He spoke quietly, all gruffness gone from his voice. In its smooth timbre Miranda heard echoes of exotic worlds, hard realities and a loneliness she understood all to well.

"Hawke—" She wasn't sure what she meant to say, how she planned to finish. Before she had a chance to figure it out, the high-pitched shriek of sirens rent the air.

She jumped, her hands tightening on the steering wheel, her gaze flying to the rearview mirror. Lights flashed in the distance, brilliant against the darkness and coming fast.

"The police. They've found us." Her voice shook, her foot pressing on the gas pedal in a knee-jerk reaction that sent the car lunging forward.

"Ease up, babe. Speeding will just call attention to us." Hawke rested a hand on her shoulder, his palm warm through her T-shirt.

"Call attention to us? They're right on our tail." And getting closer every minute.

"No. They're not. They're on the way somewhere else. We just happen to be between them and where they're heading."

"You can't know that."

"No, I can't. But this car's not registered in my name. There's no way they can know I'm in it. All we have to do is slow down and pull out of their way."

"But—"

"Babe, my neck is at stake here, too. Pull over and get out of the way before they start wondering why we're speeding ahead of them." His words were calm, but there was underlying tension to them. Not fear. Something else. Frustration. Worry. Anger.

She nodded, easing her foot off the pedal, forcing herself to pull to the shoulder as the police cars sped toward them. The sirens crested to a screaming frenzy, lights flashing their dire warning. Every muscle in Miranda's body tensed, her mind shouting that she should get out and run while she had the chance.

If Hawke was wrong, if…

In a wild, shrieking chorus, three police cruisers sped by, their lights illuminating the car, then leaving it in darkness once again. Silence settled over the night, the hushed chug of the engine a quiet backdrop to the racing beat of Miranda's heart. She knew she should pull back onto the highway, get the car moving again, but she was shaking so hard she wasn't sure she could manage it.

"They're gone now. You're safe." Hawke's voice was a whispered breath against her ear, his fingers stroking down her arm and capturing her hand, his palm warm against her clammy skin. His touch much too comforting for her peace of mind. "Everything is all right."

"No, it isn't." She took a deep breath, tugged her hand from his and pressed down on the accelerator. "I'm with a man I don't know, driving hundreds of miles from home so that I can catch a ride to a country halfway around the world. The police think I'm a murderer. Some drug dealer I've never had any contact with wants me dead. My nephew…" She shook her head, stopped herself before her sorrow could take wing. "It's *not* all right."

Hawke figured it would be better not to argue the point. Mostly because Miranda was right. While they might be all right for now, there was no telling how long that would last. "No, but we're safe for the time being. That's something to be thankful for."

She shrugged, taking one hand off the steering wheel and rubbing at the base of her neck, the bicep in her arm firm beneath pale, silky skin. Hawke resisted the urge to brush her hand away and feel the strong line of her neck under his palm, the softness of her hair against his knuckles. That would be a mistake. One he couldn't afford to make.

"Telling me we're safe for the time being doesn't make me feel safe at all."

"Then what will?"

"Waking up to find this is all a nightmare." Her voice shook, the hollows beneath her eyes darkly shadowed. For the second time that evening and probably only the second time in a decade, Hawke felt the hard edge of guilt nudging at him, telling him he'd gotten an innocent woman into the kind of danger she might not survive.

"If I could make that happen for you, I would. But I can't."

"Then I guess I'll just have to keep driving and pray we both manage to make it through this alive."

"You may want to keep me off that request, babe. God might be more willing to answer."

She glanced in his direction, the curiosity in her eyes unmistakable, but she didn't ask what he meant. Maybe she already knew. "God doesn't play favorites. He'll watch out for us equally."

"Maybe." Hawke's head was pounding too hard for him to engage in philosophical debate. Besides, while religion wasn't his thing, he'd experienced enough of life to believe there was something more to it than what could be seen; that a power greater than his own will and strength existed. What he had yet to decide was whether or not that equated to a loving God who took a personal interest in His creations.

"Sometimes I have a hard time understanding it all. How He works. Why He answers some prayers with a yes, others with a no, but I guess what it boils down to is faith. Just believing that no matter what happens, He's there." Miranda spoke so softly Hawke barely heard the quiet words that seemed more for herself than for him.

This time he gave into temptation and slid his hand under the thick weight of her hair, his palm resting on the silky skin at the nape of her neck. "Someone like you never need worry that God won't be there."

She glanced his way, her eyes shadowed. "Like I said, neither does someone like you."

She didn't seem to expect a response and Hawke didn't give one. Instead, he let the silence of the night and the darkness beyond the windows envelop them.

SIX

Home. The word danced through Miranda's mind as the first glimmer of dawn streaked the horizon. She'd wound her way through the Blue Ridge mountains, stopping only once to get gas with a credit card Hawke fished from his glove compartment. The name on it was unfamiliar and, according to Hawke, untraceable. Miranda supposed she should have found comfort in that, but the longer the night had stretched on, the more the idea of returning home appealed.

Last night, she'd been desperate to escape the empty house and Lauren. Now, she'd give anything to step into the bright yellow kitchen, listen to her sister's footsteps on the tile.

And she could.

Hawke's eyes were closed, the gun peeking out from beneath the T-shirt he wore. All it would take was one quick yank and it would be in her hands. She could use Hawke's cell phone to call the police. Then wait somewhere until they arrived. If she could have imagined a good outcome, she might have attempted it, but all she could picture was a cold jail cell and a quick brutal death.

"What are you thinking?" Hawke broke into her thoughts and Miranda jerked, hoping guilt wasn't written all over her face.

"That I want to go home."

"To your sister and brother?"

"They don't live with me."

"Then what is home to you? A house? A community?"

"Justin. But he's no longer there, so I guess my job. My routine. My life the way it was before."

"Before last night?"

"Before Justin died."

He nodded. "I think many people have times they'd like to go back to."

"Even you?"

"Even me." He didn't seem inclined to elaborate and Miranda told herself she should let the subject drop. After all, this wasn't a casual conversation between friends or an intimate discussion with a man she was dating. Hawke was a stranger, a man she didn't know and wasn't sure she trusted.

She stole a quick glance at his profile—the hard line of his jaw, the scar that bisected his cheek—and couldn't keep herself from asking the questions she knew she shouldn't. "What times do you wish you could go back to?"

His mouth curved in a half smile and he shrugged. "Right now, I'll just settle for getting back to Thailand."

"Do you have family there?"

"A brother. I haven't seen him in almost a year."

"You must be happy that you'll be seeing him soon, then."

"I won't be happy until I know he's safe."

"Do you think he's not?"

"He should be, but what should be isn't always what is. The fact that you're here with me is a perfect example of that. You should be home safe. Instead, you're running for your life." He paused, reached for the pack that sat in the backseat and rifled through it, pulling out a bottle of aspirin.

"Still have a headache?"

"If you can call a sledgehammer in your skull that, yeah." He swallowed three pills dry and recapped the bottle. "But I'll live. That's our exit. We're looking for a church outside of town."

The switch in topic was so sudden Miranda almost missed it *and* her turn. She swerved toward the exit just in time, taking the off-ramp too quickly. The car fishtailed, sliding toward the shoulder as Miranda gripped the steering wheel and tried to remember what she'd heard about reacting to a spin. Should she slam on the breaks? Jerk the steering wheel toward the spin? Away from it?

Her sleep-deprived brain couldn't hold on to a thought long enough to react and she was sure whatever she did would be wrong.

Hawke's shoulder pressed into hers, his hands clamping over Miranda's, his stubble-covered jaw rubbing against hers. "You're okay. It's okay."

The car straightened and Miranda let out the breath she hadn't realized she'd been holding. Her hands were slick on the wheel, her pulse pounding, her body shaking so hard she was sure Hawke could feel the vibration of her fear.

"No, it's not okay. *I'm* not okay." She whispered the words, not meaning for Hawke to respond, but he did, his hand cupping her shoulder, his touch warm and more comforting than it should have been.

"It will be okay and you will be, too. I promise."

"Promises are a dime a dozen." She'd heard them all before—from her mother, her father, her sister. From every man she'd ever dated. And she'd believed them all until, one after another, they'd been broken.

"Not mine. I never make a promise I don't intend to keep." The gruff assurance in his voice held a dark edge, but his hand remained gentle, his fingers brushing against the exposed skin near the neckline of Miranda's shirt, their warmth easing her shivers of fear.

For a moment, she allowed herself to believe his words, to accept his comforting touch. Only the knowledge that she'd done so before with people she'd known better and trusted more, kept her from leaning into his touch, accepting his assurance.

"'He means well' is useless unless he does well." She muttered the dark reminder, the words acid on her tongue.

"Plautus."

She glanced his way, surprised. "That's right."

"Here is one for you, then—'He who promises more than he is able to perform is false to himself; and he who does not perform what he has promised, is a traitor to his friend.'"

"George Shelley. But we're not friends."

"We will be. Besides, I am never false to myself. If I didn't believe I could get you home safely, I would take a chance and leave you here with my friend and his family."

"You could leave me here anyway."

"It would be too dangerous. For you and for them. Noah's wife is expecting a baby soon. His mind is on other things. Being distracted from a mission is the first step to death."

"Another quote?"

"Yeah. From Hawke Morran's guide to survival."

"You know a lot about survival?"

"I know *everything* about survival. If I didn't, I'd have been dead a hundred times over." His hand slipped from her shoulder and Miranda shivered—whether from the cool air that slid across her skin or from his words, she didn't know.

"It sounds like you live a dangerous life."

"Did you think otherwise?" His tone was clipped and he leaned forward, staring out into the hazy morning light, his tension filling the car, seeping into Miranda's already taut nerves.

She clenched her jaw against the tremors that raced through her and tried to keep her voice calm. "What's wrong?"

"It's quiet."

"It's six in the morning. It's supposed to be quiet."

"Not like this. Something is off."

Miranda liked the sound of that about as much as she liked trusting a man she didn't know. "What?"

"Maybe a trap. Maybe just me being overcautious. Pull over."

"What? Where?" The road was narrow, too narrow to stop the car safely even if she pulled as far over as she could.

"The cornfield. Drive into it and stop the car."

"But—"

"Are we destined to waste all our time arguing, Miranda? Or can you, just this once, do things my way without a fight?"

"I don't argue and I'm not a fighter." To prove her point, Miranda did as he suggested, the bumping thump of the car as she pulled deep into the field making her wish she'd stuck to her guns and stayed the course. She shut off the engine and turned to face Hawke, the sudden silence eerie. "There. Happy now?"

"Not yet. Let's wait a while."

"If we wait too long, we'll miss our ride."

"If we walk into a trap, we won't need a ride and all the planning my friend has done will be wasted."

"The best laid plans—"

"—of mice and men. Enough quotes. Listen to me." He leaned in, placing a hand on each of Miranda's shoulders, staring into her eyes with such grim determination she was sure she wasn't going to like what he had to say. "The church is close. Maybe three miles. We're to meet my friend there in less than an hour. I'm going to jog in. Make sure it's safe. If it is, we'll be back for you by seven-thirty. If we aren't, cut through the cornfield until you find another road. Then get out of town."

"And go where?"

"Somewhere no one can find you."

"No way. There isn't a place like that. Besides, you can't run three miles with that head injury."

"Watch me." Before Miranda could even react, Hawke opened the door and stepped out of the car.

"Wait!" She scrambled across the car seat, panic giving her wings, and grabbed his hand. "I'll come with you."

"You ever run three miles before?"

"Maybe. In high school."

"And that was how long ago? Six years? Seven?"

"Twelve. But that doesn't mean I can't do it now." The coolness of the morning wrapped around her, the corn stalks whispering secrets to the sky, to the earth, to anyone who cared to hear—life and death written into the soil that fed them and singing into the air with every swaying movement. If someone came while Hawke was gone, Miranda's blood could be spilled onto the earth as easily as Abel's had thousands of years ago, seeping into the ground and feeding the plants with only God as witness to what had happened.

She shuddered and straightened her spine, doing her best to look strong, invincible and completely unafraid.

Hawke wasn't buying it. She could see it in the half smile that softened the grim lines of his face. "Sorry, babe, but I'd have to disagree. You're not made for running."

"I'm made for whatever I put my mind to."

"That I *can* agree with, but I've got to move fast. You won't be able to keep up. Stay here. It's safer for both of us."

He took a step away, tugging at her hold on his hand. She refused to release her grip, afraid of what might happen if he disappeared and didn't come back. "I can keep up."

"You're afraid, but you don't have to be. I told you I'd make sure you were all right." He spoke quietly, moving in close, pulling her forward until her head rested against his chest. She could hear the solid beat of his heart, the quiet inhalations of each breath and, despite the warnings that screamed through her, she let her arms slip around his waist, let herself cling to the comfort he offered.

"That's going to be hard for you to do if you aren't around."

"Weren't you saying last night that God doesn't play favorites? That He'll look after us both?"

"Yes, but—"

"So believe it and stop being afraid."

She nodded her head, tried to pull back and look up into Hawke's face, but his arms tightened around her as if he were as reluctant to leave as she was to let him go. He ran a hand over her hair, smoothing the curly wayward strands Miranda knew must be tangled and knotted. "Okay now?"

She nodded again, and he released his hold, stepping away, his eyes storm-cloud gray, his expression grim. "Good. Now, get back in the car. I've got to hurry."

Miranda was about to do as Hawke suggested when the sound of an engine broke the morning silence. Her heart skipped a beat, and she grabbed for Hawke's hand again. "Someone's coming."

"We're not the only people awake this morning. There are plenty of reasons someone might be on the road." Hawke didn't sound nearly as convinced as Miranda would have liked him to be, and he turned toward the road, his free hand dropping to the gun that peeked out from under his T-shirt.

Whoever it was, whatever the vehicle, it was close now, roaring along the quiet road just out of sight. Then, as suddenly as it had started the sound ceased, the sudden silence deafening.

Miranda's breath caught in her throat, her heart slamming so hard she thought it would burst from her chest.

Hawke turned his head, met her gaze, mouthing a command for her to hide.

She nodded, but couldn't bring herself to leave.

Hawke was armed, but injured. There was no way she
planned to hide while he fought off their faceless
enemy, no matter how scared she was.

Leaves crackled and something scuffled just out of
sight. Miranda jumped, nearly falling backward as a
dark figure stepped into view.

The gun was in Hawke's hand so quickly, Miranda
didn't even see him move. She gasped, backing up then
moving closer. Not sure if she wanted to tell him to stop,
or encourage him to shoot.

"I wouldn't come any closer." He growled the words,
the menace in them unmistakable and enough to stop
the approaching figure.

"I guess I've found the right party." If the speaker was
surprised by the gun or worried by it he didn't let it show.

"Not by a long shot, so why don't you go back the
way you came and forget you ever saw us?" Hawke
took a step forward and Miranda shadowed him, squint-
ing to see the person they were approaching.

"Because a friend asked for my help and I agreed to
give it. He's counting on me. So are you, I think." He
took a step closer and Miranda could make out shaggy
light brown hair and even features. He didn't look in-
timidating, though she was sure that didn't mean much.

"Stay where you are and tell me your story. Fast."

"I'm a friend of Noah's. His pastor, actually. He
couldn't make it to meet you, so he sent me."

"Couldn't make it?"

"He was waylaid by some unhappy federal agents.
I've been driving up and down this road for an hour,
hoping I'd catch you before you made it to the church.
Lakeview is crawling with agents and state cops. They
haven't made it as far as Grace Christian, but it's just a

matter of time before they do. Better that we meet here. If they find you at the church, they'll know Noah sent you there. I don't think either of us want that."

"I'd rather not be found at all." Hawke lowered the gun, locking the safety again. He didn't sense danger from the man standing before him and he trusted his instincts much more than he trusted a stranger's words.

"Then we'd better get you out of town fast."

"Just like that you agree to help a suspected felon?" Despite his gut instinct about the man, Hawke wasn't sure he was buying the story.

"Just like that I agreed to help a friend help a friend."

"Why?"

"Because Noah is a man of strong convictions. I trust him. When his wife called me from her veterinary clinic and explained what was going on, I knew I had to help. I'm Ben Avery, by the way." He held out a hand, completely ignoring the gun Hawke still held.

"A pastor."

"Yes."

"You look military to me." Hawke could spot one a mile away and this guy reeked special forces, his stance relaxed, but alert, his balance ready for a quick shift to attack if need be.

"*Was* military. That was a long time ago."

The fact that he admitted it said something about the man. People lied when they had something to hide. The truth was a luxury reserved for the innocent. He nodded, slid the gun out of sight. "Okay. What's the plan?"

"Noah wanted to have a pilot friend fly you out to California, but the feds are nosing around everyone he knows and we can't risk it. I've called in a favor. A missionary brush pilot who retired a few years back. He's got a plane and a license and can fly you out west. There will be someone waiting at the airport with your passports and identification."

Hawke shook his head, fingering the scar that bisected his cheek. "Passports and identification or not, this'll be hard to hide from airport security."

"Not with the right tools." Ben smiled. "Disguise is something I know a little about. Stay here. I'll get my stuff."

Hawke grabbed Ben's arm as he turned away, felt hard muscles beneath flannel. The guy might be ex-military, but he was still trained and ready to fight.

"If you double-cross me…." He let the words trail off, let the threat hang in the air.

"I've got nothing to gain from it and everything to lose. I've made a life in Lakeview. A good one. I'm not going to risk it by alerting the feds to the fact that I'm aiding a felon. Now, let's get this done. You've got to be at an airstrip outside of Charlottesville in three hours. From there you head to California as honeymooners." He shot a glance in Miranda's direction and shrugged. "It was the easiest cover we could come up with. Now, are we ready to go?"

Hawke hesitated. Trust or not? It's what everything in his life eventually boiled down to. He stared into Ben's eyes, trying to find truth or falsehood there. All he saw was compassion and the strange knowledge he'd often seen in Noah Stone's eyes, a knowledge that seemed a reflection of much more than human understanding and that seemed to beg Hawke to believe in things he'd refused for much too long.

He dropped Ben's arm and stepped back. "Go get

what you need and let's get moving before someone else finds us here."

Ben smiled, the tension in his jaw and shoulders the only hint of what he was feeling, then stepped back into the shadows, disappearing as quickly as he had come and leaving Hawke with the strange feeling that things were about to change. That his life perspective was about to be challenged, that what he'd always believed might not be the truth and that what he'd sensed so many times and ignored had hooked its claws into him and was not about to let go. Good or bad. Righteous or evil. Something was tugging at his soul and Hawke wondered just how long he'd be able to ignore.

A while longer, anyway. He had a mission to fulfill. Deep thinking and soul-searching would have to wait until he completed it.

He turned to Miranda, grabbing her hand, squeezing gently. Her skin was milk-white in the morning light, the freckles on her nose and cheeks standing out in stark contrast. He'd thought her hair brown, but now he could see hints of fiery red and butterscotch yellow in its depth. Dark circles shadowed her eyes, giving her a fragile, wounded appearance. The fierce need to protect her reared up, taking Hawke by surprise. She'd saved his life and Hawke believed in repaying what was owed. Emotional involvement had never played into it before. He couldn't let it now, either. Doing so could only distract him from his goal.

"Is he telling the truth?" She whispered the words, her gaze fixed on the spot where Ben had disappeared.

"Probably."

"Probably? I don't think I like the way that sounds."

"I don't like it, either, but it's all we've got right now."

Miranda opened her mouth to respond, but crackling grass and breaking cornstalks announced Ben's return, the purposeful warning designed to keep Hawke from pulling his gun again. Obviously, the man was savvy about survival. What remained to be seen was whether or not he was as trustworthy as he claimed. Only time would tell that.

Unfortunately, Hawke and Miranda didn't have much of it left. Danger was breathing down Hawke's neck. He could feel it. If they didn't get out of Lakeview soon, they wouldn't get out at all.

And that just wasn't an option.

Hand on his gun, Hawke strode toward the approaching man.

SEVEN

Forty hours of flying was enough to convince Miranda that staying in one place for a lifetime wasn't entirely a bad thing. Gritty-eyed from hours of fitful sleep, skin layered with grime, she stared out the window of the 747 as the ground rose up to meet it. With a bump and thump of protest, the plane landed, the landscape speeding by in a dizzying array of colors. In a matter of minutes, she and Hawke would depart from the relative safety of the plane. Just the thought made her heart race and her breath hitch.

"Relax, sweetheart," Hawke's arm slipped around her shoulder, his lips pressing into her hair. "We've been looking forward to this trip for months. You should be excited, not terrified."

The words were a subtle warning and Miranda tried to respond, pushing back strands of stick-straight hair and smiling.

"I *am* excited." And not nearly as good an actor as Hawke. Her words sounded phony, her smile felt forced. She'd have to do better if they were going to make it out of the airport without calling attention to themselves.

"Me, too." Hawke's hand smoothed over her arm, his gaze as warm and loving as any newlywed's should be. "Two weeks alone together is exactly what we need after so many months of wedding preparations. I've missed spending time with you."

His words were meant to carry and they did. The elderly woman seated next to him sighed, smiling at Miranda. "You're a very fortunate young woman to have a such a romantic husband."

Miranda tried to return the smile, praying she'd be as convincing as Hawke had been during the long flight. "I know I am."

She leaned her head against his shoulder, felt the taut muscles and coiled strength beneath the jacket he wore. Brown contacts had turned his smoky eyes dark, and a plasticky substance disguised his scar. With his hair down, his cheeks were less prominent, his face less granite and more smooth-planed. He looked model-handsome, clean-cut and nothing like the hardened criminal he could have passed for when they'd first met. Perfect husband material. Just like he was supposed to be.

Miranda's appearance had changed, too. Her curly hair was covered by a black wig that looked so natural she was sure it was made of real hair, her lips tinged with red, her freckles covered with makeup and her cheekbones hollowed with blush. She looked older, more worldly; the kind of woman who'd marry the kind of man Hawke looked to be.

It was no wonder the elderly woman believed their story.

She just hoped the people at customs would. Unlike the other airports they'd passed through, this one was sure to have been alerted to Hawke and Miranda's possible arrival. It wouldn't take much to give them away.

Passengers rose to grab bags and belongings, and Hawke squeezed Miranda's shoulder as if he could offer her the confidence she lacked. "This is it. Ready for the adventure?" There was warmth and humor in his voice, but his eyes flashed with impatience. No doubt he was anxious to get on with things.

Miranda, on the other hand, was not. She nodded anyway, praying that God would get them through this airport the same way He had the others they'd been through—quick, easy, no hassle. "Of course. Let's do it."

Hawke's half smile eased some of the impatience from his eyes, but Miranda still had the impression of banked fires, ready to burst to life if given the opportunity. He grabbed her hand, pulling her into the aisle behind him, the elderly woman chatting with him as they exited the plane.

It all seemed so normal, Miranda could almost believe she and Hawke were no longer in danger. Almost.

Somehow she managed to say goodbye to the older woman, exchanging a brief hug and well-wishes. Then she followed Hawke into the airport, watched as he collected the suitcase filled with clothes that Ben's friend had provided, allowed herself to be tugged toward customs. All around her the building teemed with life, bursting at the seams and ready to embrace all who came. Smiles. Everywhere. Dark eyes, dark hair, white teeth flashing in tanned faces. Hawke's home and a world away from anything Miranda had ever experienced.

In other circumstances she might have enjoyed the newness, but now she could only feel terror and a deep-seated emptiness, her heart heavy with what she'd lost and what she might still lose. To never see Lauren again, never see Max, her friends, her church, seemed a distinct possibility. She had the sudden urge to confess all to the first English-speaking authority she met, to beg for help. Someone, somewhere should be able to convince the DEA that she and Hawke were innocent.

As if he sensed her thoughts, Hawke released his grip on her hand and wound his arm around her waist, tugging her close to his side. His leather jacket was cool against her cheek, the scent of earth and sun clinging to it despite the hours they'd spent on airplanes and in airports. "Now's not the time to panic, babe. We're almost home free. There will be people watching for us and they're trained to notice body language. Try to relax and look like you're enjoying yourself."

"I've never been much of an actress." All the drama and acting ability had been passed from her mother to her sister, leaving Miranda with an even-keeled temperament and little ability to fake emotions she didn't feel. Or hide those she did.

"You better learn quick, then, because we're about a hundred yards from an agent."

"Where?" Miranda's heart nearly leaped from her chest, and she stumbled, with only Hawke's strong hold keeping her from falling flat on her face.

"Standing on the other side of customs. Leaning against the wall. Don't even think about looking for him. You've got eyes only for me. We're newlyweds, remember?" His voice was a soft caress as his hand came up to cup her cheek, his eyes staring into hers as if she were the most beautiful woman he'd ever seen. If she hadn't known the truth of their situation, if she'd been simply an observer watching as she and Hawke approached customs, she'd be convinced that the man beside her was completely besotted.

She nodded, trying desperately to get into character. Unfortunately, every man she'd ever cared about had been a liar, a cheat or both, and the only emotion she could dredge up was fear. "Do you think he's noticed us?"

"Not yet, but if you keep looking like a deer in the headlights it'll only be a matter of time before he does."

"I told you I'm not a good actress."

"Then I guess I'll have to compensate." Before she knew what he'd planned, Hawke whirled her into his arms and kissed her. The contact was brief, a quick press of his lips to hers. Something that should have been nothing, but felt like much more. Electricity. Chemistry. All the things she would have wanted if they were a real couple on a real honeymoon.

Her cheeks heated and she had to resist the urge to press her fingers to her lips.

Hawke seemed unfazed by the contact, his arm wrapping around her waist once again, his focus on the customs official who was waving them forward. "Hand me your passport, babe."

She pulled it from her purse, trying to still the fine tremors that raced through her, trying to calm the wild racing of her heart.

Hawke handed the man both passports, smiling down at Miranda as the documents were checked and stamped.

"Do you have anything to claim?" The official's

words were deeply accented, his eyes dark brown and blank—he asked the question a thousand times a day and probably expected nothing out of the ordinary.

"No." Hawke's own accent had slipped away, replaced by a Texas drawl that made Miranda wince. Obviously, he had no formal training in voice disguise, but the customs official didn't seem bothered by it. He stamped the passports, waving Hawke and Miranda through and turning his attention to the next person in line.

One down. One more to go.

Miranda was sure she felt eyes spearing into her as she and Hawke sauntered away. The tension in Hawke's arm told her he felt it, too, and she met his gaze, saw the warning there.

Please God, don't let us get stopped now.

The prayer chanted through her mind, her feet moving by rote, one plodding step at a time. Her body felt disconnected from the fear that thrummed along her nerves. Shouldn't adrenaline be pumping through her, adding a burst of energy to her flagging reserves? She was sure it should, but there was nothing. Not even a little oomph to help her move more quickly.

"You okay, darlin'?" Hawke spoke loudly, his drawl attracting attention from half a dozen people.

"Just tired." She hoped that was the response he was looking for.

"You sure? 'Cause you're lookin' a little green around the gills. If you need to use the little girl's room it's right down this hall." If the situation hadn't been so serious, the implications of his words so frightening, Miranda might have laughed at his suddenly overdone acting.

As it was, she was sure she was turning the greenish hue he'd mentioned, fear pulsing through her as she realized what Hawke must be trying to tell her—they'd been spotted. "I *am* feeling a little queasy. You know what a bad traveler I am."

"You'll feel better once we get settled in." He steered her toward a corridor as he spoke, his hand hard against her waist. "Looks like the restroom is right down this hall. Come on."

He pulled her into a narrow corridor marked with restroom and pay-phone signs, led her a few steps into the dimly lit hall, then dropped his hold on their suitcase, his arm slipping from her waist, his hand claiming hers. "Run!"

Before she could catch her breath, think things through, decide what Hawke's plan was, they were racing down the hall toward what looked like an emergency exit, slamming into it, forcing it open. A high-pitched shriek split the air, the sound of screams and footfall echoing into the corridor. Chaos followed them into bright sunlight and buzzing traffic, honking horns and thick, humid air. Miranda could barely breath, whether from fear or from the moisture hanging so heavy around her, she didn't know. Her heart slammed in time with her pounding feet, her breath gasping from searing lungs.

And they ran on, past startled street vendors and waving taxi drivers, turning one corner after another, moving from affluence to squalor, from suits to rags, running on and on until Miranda was sure her heart would burst with the effort.

She stumbled, her foot catching on cracked pavement, and skidded onto her knees, pain slicing through her as Hawke yanked her back upright, barely breaking his stride.

"Come on, babe. You said you could run three miles. Prove it." He growled the words, his grip on her hand painfully tight.

"I didn't think I'd have to do it at this fast a pace." She panted the words out, her anger at Hawke and at her weakness, at the situation making her grit her teeth and move faster.

"We do what we have to do to survive." He yanked her down a dank alley, slowing his pace from a dead run to a jog. Still, Miranda couldn't catch her breath, couldn't get her heartbeat to slow. Of all the ways to die, this would be the last she'd ever imagine for herself—collapsing from heart failure in a back alley in Southeast Asia.

Things slithered and scurried in the dark shadows, the sounds carrying above Miranda's gasps and the pounding of shoes against pavement. Snakes, rats, huge spiders, Miranda imagined any and all lurking just out of sight. None were quite as bad as what she imagined might be coming behind her. Men. With guns. Men who wanted her dead.

The thought alone was enough to keep her going.

Finally, Hawke stopped, glancing behind and ahead before approaching a run-down apartment building. "This is it."

"Home?"

"Of a sort."

"You don't think the DEA will be waiting for you here?"

"They don't know about it. Come on. We can get supplies and call for a ride." He tugged her up crumbling cement steps and into the dark lobby of the building. The water-stained red carpet must have once been lush and thick, but now looked dingy and old, the mildewy scent that emanated from it thick enough to make Miranda's eyes water.

She coughed, her empty stomach rebelling, her vision swimming, the dim light fading.

"Hey, you okay?" Hawke's hands rested on her shoulders, holding her steady, his eyes staring into hers, anchoring her even more than his firm grip.

"Fine."

He didn't move, his gaze searching hers as if he might find another answer within the depth of her eyes.

The intensity of his stare lodged in Miranda's stomach and she pulled away from his hands. In the two days they'd spent traveling, she'd learned little about her companion, their conversations limited by the public nature of their transportation. She'd wondered, though, who he was, what had made him decide to take the job the DEA had offered, whether or not he was telling her the whole truth about what was going on. In the end, she'd found no answers, only a still-quiet voice that told her Hawke was her best hope for survival.

She fidgeted under his stare, brushing at the faded denim of her jeans and tugging at one long, dark lock of her phony hair. "Aren't we going to your place?"

"Only if you can make it up four flights of stairs."

"I've made it this far. I can make it a little farther."

"Good." He started up, and Miranda followed behind, the scuffed wood railing and paint-peeling walls closing in on her as she hurried up one flight after another. At any moment she expected to hear sounds of pursuit, a door slamming open, footfall, gunshots. But besides her own gasping breath and the pad of her shoes and Hawke's, the building seemed empty.

By the time they reached the fourth-floor landing, she was ready to collapse, her wobbly knees and shaking legs making her wish she'd kept up the exercise program she'd started at the beginning of the year. Next year she'd do better. If she survived that long.

Hawke grabbed her hand, pulling her to a stop. "Wait here. I'm going to check things out."

"What things?" Miranda's heart skipped a beat at the look in his eyes. "You think someone is waiting for us?"

"If I did, we wouldn't be here, but I'm still going to check." Hawke could tell by the look on Miranda's face that she didn't like the idea of waiting around while he did recon, but he planned to do it anyway. Anything else would be a foolish risk. He'd come too far to get caught now.

She shifted from foot to foot, the dark wig she wore framing a face that was gaunt with fear and fatigue. Despite that, despite her obvious stress, her skin was flawless, her cheeks pink with exertion. Her lips…

He stopped the thought cold. Kissing her in the airport had seemed a good idea. Until he'd done it. Now he was doing his best to forget the touch of her lips against his. Thinking about the softness of her mouth was *not* the way to do that.

"Stay here." There was more force to his words than necessary, anger at what he'd done making his voice harsh.

If she noticed, Miranda didn't seem to care. Her hand fisted around his wrist. "We can go together."

"And risk getting caught together? You stay here. I'll come back for you if it's clear."

"And if you don't?"

"Then you need to find your way to Mae Hong Son." It's where his home was, the only place he ever felt truly safe. If she made it there, his team would take care of her. *If.* Miranda knew nothing about Thailand, nothing about who she could trust and who she couldn't. Without him, she'd be lost.

So, he'd just have make sure she didn't have to be without him.

Her compassion for a stranger had gotten her into this mess. His determination would get her out of it.

He hoped.

Hawke grimaced, raking his hair back from his forehead. The pounding pain in his head had faded hours ago; the dull ache that replaced it was more tolerable. Adrenaline hummed through his veins, stealing exhaustion. Here on his home turf, he knew the rules, knew how to play the game. All he had to do was stay one step ahead of his enemies. And that's exactly what he planned to do.

"Do what I say and stay here." He threw the words over his shoulder as he pushed open the door that led to the fourth-floor hallway. There were apartments on either side of the long, narrow space. All had been abandoned years ago, their doors yawning open into debris-littered rooms. Even here in one of the more derelict sections of Bangkok, money could be made from renting out the space. Hawke had no desire to do so. The occupied apartments on the lower levels were for those who had no other place to go. Women mostly. Though a few men were there, as well. Displaced, homeless, but all with families who depended on them. Hawke had given them a place to stay. In return, they kept an eye on the property. If there'd been trouble here, one of the occupants would have posted a lookout and warned him before he arrived. Still, it didn't pay to take chances and he approached the one closed door on the floor with caution, his fingers itching to wrap around the gun he'd had to leave in the States.

The door was locked just as he he'd left it nine months ago. He used his key, shoving the door open with one hand, his body pressed close to the wall. No barrage of bullets followed, no whisper of sound or pinprick of warning along his nerves. He waited anyway, his body still as death, everything inside him straining for out-of-place sounds, shifting shadows. Five minutes passed. Then seven. When nothing moved, he went in low, his gaze scanning the room. No furniture. No closets. Nowhere for someone to hide. Just the way he'd planned it.

He moved around a corner and into the empty kitchen and found no sign that his safe house had been discovered. He hadn't expected it to be. He'd told no one about the place. Not his brother and not any of his men. Betrayal could come from the most trusted ally. Even family. He'd learned that lesson too late to save his parents and sister. It was one he would never forget.

He shook aside thoughts of the past, refusing to allow distraction. One moment of hesitation, one second of inattention could cost a man his life. Another well-learned lesson. One he'd been lucky to survive.

Lucky?

The question whispered through his mind as it had so many times since the day six years ago when Noah

Stone had saved his life. The jungles of Mae Hong Son weren't a place where men ran into each other. Yet somehow Noah had found Hawke lying nearly dead in the summer overgrowth.

The past again. It seemed to haunt him these last few days. Perhaps it was Miranda, her quiet resolve and obvious normality reminding Hawke of all he'd lost. Or perhaps it was his own need for something more than the life he'd made that had him dwelling on the times better forgotten. Whatever the case, he couldn't afford the distraction.

He grabbed the doorknob to the only bedroom in the apartment. Locked. Just as he'd left it. He used a second key to unlock the door. He pulled it open, his gaze dropping. A thin white thread stretched across the doorway a foot above the floor.

Hawke smiled, relaxing for the first time in days.

Unlike the rest of the apartment, this room was furnished with a bed, a desk, a computer, a dresser and a chair. To the left, a door opened into the apartment's only bathroom. To the right, a closed door concealed the supplies Hawke needed. He moved quickly, unlocking the closet door and the metal safe within it, pulling out the gun and ammo he kept there, a handful of cash and coins and a cell phone. He'd call Simon, make sure his younger brother was staying out of trouble, then call one of his men to arrange transportation.

He pushed speed dial, pulling on a shoulder harness while the phone rang. "Come on, Si, pick up." Hawke muttered the words as he strode back across the room, a sense of urgency feeding his steps. Miranda was waiting. Hopefully in exactly the place he'd left her.

The phone continued to ring, no answering machine and no answer, until Hawke finally hung up. There was something wrong. Really wrong.

A sound carried on the still air, a whisper of movement just out of sight. Hawke eased up against the wall, the gun in his hand a familiar friend, adrenaline coursing through him as it had so often in the past ten years. This was his life. What he had become. What it seemed he would always be. A man one mistake away from death.

Another sound followed the first, a brush of fabric against the wall or the soft sigh of someone's breath. Hawke stayed put, letting the intruder come to him, listening to the air, feeling the slight disturbance of another's presence even before he saw the dark shape rounding the corner.

And then he didn't wait any longer. He lunged.

EIGHT

Miranda would have screamed if she'd had time, but she didn't. One minute she was creeping through a seemingly empty apartment, the next she was tackled, a full-body collision that would have sent her sprawling if a hand hadn't clamped around her waist, yanking her upright.

"Are you crazy?" Hawke's shout penetrated her terror and Miranda's legs went weak with relief.

"You didn't come back. I thought you'd passed out." Or been injured. Or worse.

"I told you to stay where you were." Hawke's eyes blazed with fury, a muscle in his jaw twitching.

"You didn't tell me how long to wait." Her own anger reared up. "If you had, I wouldn't have had to come looking."

"You could have gotten yourself *killed*." He released his hold on her waist, waved a gun near her face. "This isn't a toy. We're not playing a game. Mistakes like you just made cost lives. Do you understand?"

Miranda's eyes were riveted to the gun, her throat so tight she couldn't speak. She nodded instead, the movement jerky. Death had never been something to fear, though now, in the face of what might have happened, Miranda desperately wanted to avoid it.

"Good, because I didn't come into this mission planning to lose you. From now on you stay where I leave you. I can't spend the next few days worrying that every noise I hear might be you. Hesitation kills. I can't afford to hesitate." His voice softened as he spoke, the muscles in his jaw relaxing.

He traced a line down her jaw, lifting her chin and peering into her eyes. "Come sit down on the bed. You look like you're about to keel over."

Miranda didn't argue as he urged her down onto a soft comforter. Her legs were weak, her mind empty. "I'm sorry. I guess I wasn't thinking."

"Sure you were. You were thinking about me. Next time, think about yourself." He shoved the gun into the holster he now wore, pulled his hair back at the nape of his neck, grabbed clothes from a dresser and a backpack from a closet, his movements methodical and easy, as if he'd performed them a thousand times before.

"Are we going somewhere?"

"*I'm* going somewhere. You're staying here until I get back."

"I don't think I like that idea."

"Babe, there hasn't been an idea of mine yet that you have." He shot her a crooked grin, pulled a cell phone from his pocket. "I'm going to call my brother and arrange a ride for us. Then I've got some business to attend to in Bangkok. The safest place for you is here."

Miranda wanted to argue, but doing so would only be a waste of time. The sooner Hawke left and came back, the sooner they could find the person who'd set him up and Miranda could return home. "All right."

He cocked an eyebrow, leaned a shoulder against the wall and watched Miranda through dark eyes. "All right? Will it be that simple this time?"

"I'm too tired to do anymore running."

He straightened, crossed the room, his hand brushing over the wig Miranda still wore and coming to rest on the back of her neck, the warmth of it spreading through her and making her feel safer than she had in hours. "It's been a long few days, but this will all be over soon."

"It's been a long week and I'm not sure it will ever be over."

"It'll be over. What remains to be seen is how it will end." His hand slipped away and he punched a button on the phone, raised it to his ear, his gaze never leaving Miranda.

Her cheeks heated, her heart doing a strange dance that had nothing at all to do with fear. She rose, pacing across the room and away from Hawke's too-intense stare.

"Something is wrong." He growled the words and Miranda jumped turning to face him.

"What?"

"My brother isn't answering."

"Maybe he's at work and can't pick up."

"He works for our export company. He can do just about whatever he wants. They've got him. I'm sure of it." He slammed the phone down onto the dresser, muttering under his breath as he yanked out more clothes and thrust them into the backpack.

"Maybe—"

"There is no maybe, babe. My brother's cell phone is always with him and always on. The phone I used is one I keep for emergencies. There's no way he wouldn't pick up when he saw the number on his caller ID."

"Who would take him? Green is still in the States."

"And the people he works with are here. So is the person who set me up. They think that by taking my brother they'll get me, but all they've done is sign their death certificates."

Miranda winced at the force of his words, at the violence she saw in his eyes. She'd known he could be a dangerous man, but had pushed the knowledge to the back of her mind, trying her best to convince herself that he was just like her—an innocent person drawn into something he'd never expected and hadn't asked for.

But innocence didn't look like Hawke. Or act like him.

And right now she'd be willing to believe him capable of almost anything.

She took a step toward the door, knowing how anger worked. Her father's rages had spilled out onto anyone in the vicinity. Her high school boyfriend's anger over lost basketball games, poor grades and parents, had bled into their relationship until it nearly destroyed her. Even Lauren could wound without thought when life didn't go her way. Yeah, Miranda knew *exactly* how rage worked and she had no intention of letting Hawke take his frustration out on her.

She took another step back, cleared her throat. "I'll just wait in the other room until you're done."

He stilled, his hand pausing over the open backpack as he met her gaze. "I'm scaring you."

"No, you're…" She shrugged. "Not much."

"Not much is still too much." He took a deep breath, released it, his shoulders relaxing, his fisted hands opening, the rage slowly fading from his eyes. "My brother is all the family I have left. The thought of something happening to him makes me see red."

"I understand."

"Maybe you do. It seems we've both suffered loss in our lives." He crossed the space between them, cupped her cheeks in his hands as he stared down into her eyes. "But that's not an excuse for scaring you. I'm sorry."

"Sorry? That's not a word I've heard very often from the men in my life." She meant it as a joke, something to lighten the mood, but the truth of her statement must have been in her tone.

"Then I guess you haven't had the right men in your life."

"The right men? I didn't know there were such things." She pulled away from his touch, her skin burning where his hands had been.

"There are. My friend Noah is one. His pastor is another."

"Them and not you?"

"No. Not me. But I am the right man to get you out of this mess." His half smile was self-depreciating. "I've got to go."

He stepped out of the room and Miranda followed, worry a hard, cold knot in her stomach. She wanted to beg Hawke to stay or take her with him. More than that, she wanted to close her eyes, open them again and find that everything that had happened was nothing but a bad dream. "How long will you be gone?"

"I don't know."

"Then how will I know how long to wait?"

"You'll wait an eternity if that's what it takes."

"That's not practical."

"I don't care about practical. I care about your safety.

Go wandering around this neighborhood by yourself and anything could happen. Even if it didn't, it wouldn't be long before one of the DEA's informants spotted you. If the DEA finds you, it's all over."

"Right now that doesn't seem like such a bad thing."

"It will be, babe. Someone in the DEA's office has been feeding information to drug dealers in the States. Including my name. He knows I'm here to find him. He can't afford to let that happen."

"But if you don't come back—"

"I'll come back."

"But if you don't—"

He pressed a finger against her lips, stopping her words. "Stop worrying. It'll be easy enough for me to stay hidden. Make yourself at home while I'm gone. There are clothes in the dresser. You might be able to find something that works. I wish I had food, but I cleaned everything out before I left. I'll try to grab something before I come back."

"Don't worry about it. I'm fine." She'd rather he come back sooner and skip the food. Besides, she was too nervous to eat.

"A successful mission is one in which every detail is worried about." He pulled open the door, stepped out into the hall. "I'll lock it. Don't open it for anyone."

"I won't."

"If someone knocks, ignore it. Don't get close to the door, don't make any noise. Not even a hint there's someone here."

"All right." The idea of being left behind sounded worse by the minute.

"Worse-case scenario, someone breaks down the door—"

"What?!"

"If that happens, lock the bedroom door and go out the window. There's a fire escape there."

"Hawke, I *really* don't like this idea."

"It's the best one we've got." He chucked her under her chin, stepped out into the hall. "You'll be fine."

"What about you?"

"I'll be fine, too." He didn't give her time to argue further, just closed the door with a firm click.

Miranda resisted the urge to pull it back open and watch him walk away. It wouldn't do any good and would only put off the inevitable moment when she'd be truly alone. She turned the lock and paced across the room, glancing at her watch as she did so. It was eleven o'clock in Maryland, but that didn't tell her what time it was here. What was the time difference? Ten hours? Twelve? Did it matter? She was stuck where she was until Hawke got back.

If he got back.

There was a very real possibility he wouldn't and as much as she didn't want to think about it, Miranda had to be prepared. She paced back to the door, checking the lock again, pressing her ear against the wood listening for something she hoped not to hear. All she heard was silence. She should have been relieved, but she couldn't shake the worry and dread that filled her.

"Pull yourself together and *do* something!" She muttered the command, forcing herself away from her post by the door. She'd search the bedroom, see what she could find. Maybe there were weapons, maps, tools and information she could use if Hawke didn't return. If there were, she'd find them.

Then she'd wait and pray she didn't have to use them.

NINE

Hawke didn't believe in lying and he hadn't lied to Miranda. Doing so would have been a betrayal of the strict moral code his parents had raised him with. His mother and father had both been religious people. Though there'd been no church, no Bibles to be read or studied when he was growing up, his parents had believed in God and in a cosmic balance of justice and mercy. To them, the Ten Commandments were not an arbitrary set of rules but a code of conduct to be lived by. Hawke did his best to honor their memory by doing so, though his own personal code had taken precedence more times than he was comfortable admitting.

Today had been one of those times. While he hadn't lied to Miranda, he hadn't told her the truth, either. He had no business to see to in Bangkok. None that the law would approve of anyway. But telling Miranda that he planned to blackmail a man to get the information he needed hadn't seemed like the wisest thing to do. She was worried enough without him adding more to the mix. Worse, she couldn't be counted on to stay where he'd left her. Leaving out information was the one way he could think of to keep her in place. The less she knew, the less likely she'd be to follow and intervene.

It shouldn't have bothered him, but it did. Much as he wanted to pretend that following the letter of the law made him innocent of wrongdoing, he knew the truth—a lie of omission was as serious a sin as any other. Yet, he'd done it over and over again in the past ten years. And he'd done worse.

So, why was this one small omission bothering him so much? Maybe because he was beginning to think the events of the last few days were payback. If God really did care about His creation, if He really did have a vested interested in humanity, He might just have decided it was time to balance the scales a little, give Hawke back what he'd been dishing out for the past decade—justice. Or maybe it was because the thought of lying to Miranda, of hurting her in any way, left him feeling cold.

Both were foolish thoughts, but neither would let him go as he wound his way through back alleys, skirted an upscale neighborhood and made his way to a busy tourist district. Street vendors lined the sidewalk, their stainless-steel carts reflecting watery sunlight and bright colors. The scent of sweet pastry and sticky rice made Hawke's stomach growl and his mouth water, but he'd left Miranda back at the apartment with no food. He wouldn't eat until she did.

Pay phones were easy to find on the busy thoroughfare and Hawke stepped into a booth, leaving the door open and facing the street. He was less conspicuous that way, and less vulnerable. Roaring traffic and a swarming crowd of tourists created a sea of motion that made blending in easy. All Hawke had to do was act like everyone else—and that was something he'd perfected over the years.

He pulled a baht from his pocket, slid it into the coin slot, knowing he was leaving fingerprints and not caring. The DEA and Royal Thai police already knew he was in Bangkok. Trying to hide the fact was a waste of energy. He dialed Pot o' Gold Exports first, listening as the phone rang once and a recorded message filled the line. *Closed pending DEA investigation.* Hawke slammed the phone down hot, dark anger welled up inside him—the knowledge that the message had been left for him but would be heard by clients filled him with rage. Despite his reputation for skirting the law and pursuing justice with a vengeance, Hawke had made sure the family business remained untainted, its reputation reflecting the ethical dealings of his stepfather. Now it seemed that reputation would fall victim to the same faceless enemy that had tried to have Hawke killed.

Frustration spurred him on as he picked up the phone again and dialed another number. This time to his house in Mae Hong Son. The line would be tapped, but it didn't matter. His conversation would add a little excitement to someone's boring day but would offer anyone listening nothing more than that.

"*Sawatdee khrap.*" The greeting came quickly. The soft, masculine voice was one Hawke recognized immediately.

"*Sawatdee khrap, Apirak.*"

"You're back." The Thai words sounded almost foreign after so many months of speaking and hearing only English, but they were as much Hawke's language as the ones he had learned from his stepfather. He slipped into the pattern and rhythm of Thai without conscious thought.

"Do you know why?"

"Trouble in the States. Trouble here." Apirak Koy-sayodin spit the words out, his normally smooth baritone laced with temper. Hawke's second in command and the only person besides Noah and Simon that Hawke trusted, Apirak was a master of understatements, not given to panic and loyal to a fault. If he said there was trouble, it had to be big.

"What kind of trouble is there here?"

"That hotheaded kid brother of yours got himself in deep with the DEA."

"How deep?" Hawke knew his brother could act without thinking, but couldn't imagine him being foolish enough to mess with a government agency.

"Deep enough to get carted off to jail. A couple of agents came here to question us. The one who hired you and a couple of other people. They were talking about stolen money and a murdered agent. Simon didn't take kindly to the accusations they made against you."

"What'd he do?"

"Took a swing at one of them. Gave the guy a bloody nose. He's lucky he didn't get himself shot."

"That doesn't sound like Simon."

"The agent he took a swing at had just accused the entire family of being in the Wa's pocket. The implication that your family was murdered because they double-crossed the Wa sent him over the edge."

Hawke bit back harsh words and calmed his suddenly ragged breathing. A militia group based in Myanmar, the Wa supported their guerilla efforts through drug trade. When Patrick Morran refused to ship drugs through his export business and went to the authorities with the names of men who were more willing, he, his wife and his daughter were executed by a man who had been a friend for as many years as Patrick had been in business. Hawke had been in the States obtaining an MBA. Simon had been visiting friends. Because of that, they'd lived. "The DEA knows the truth about what happened. They were taunting him for a reason."

"And he gave them a good reason to cart him off to jail. With Simon out of the picture, they probably figured you'd be easier to control, maybe even be willing to turn yourself in."

Hawke snorted. "If that's what they hope to accomplish they've made an error in judgment. I'm even more determined to stay out of their hands."

"It's more of an error in judgment than you think, Hawke." Apirak's voice warned of more bad news.

"What else?"

"Simon has disappeared."

"Disappeared?" Everything inside Hawke stilled, his nerves so alive he could hear drips of water from gutters above the street, feel the rain moving in over the city, see every speck of light and dark, each ant and roach that wove it's way between cracks in the sidewalk.

"Supposedly he escaped, but I don't believe it." Which meant Simon hadn't gone to his own safe house, hadn't used the phone he had for emergencies, had made no effort at all to make contact. Apirak didn't need to say it for Hawke to know it was true. The emergency plans they'd formulated years before were meant for times such as these. If Simon wasn't using them, it was because he wasn't able to.

Hawke's jaw was tight with worry and anger. He'd lost most of his family. He wouldn't lose Simon, too. "How long has he been gone?"

"They brought him in yesterday morning. He disappeared sometime last night."

"Any word on the street?"

"Nothing solid. Our normal informants are very quiet on this one."

"Keep listening."

"Of course." There was a second of hesitation, then Apirak spoke again. "Is the woman with you?"

"She's in a safe place." His response was vague. The less information those listening in on the conversation got, the happier Hawke would be.

"Hopefully out of sight. There have been news stories here. The tale of a mysterious and wealthy entrepreneur on the run with the sister of an American model is just too good for the press to pass up."

"I'd figured it would be."

"Just be sure you're not spotted."

"We already have been, but I'm still free."

"Make sure you keep it that way."

"I'll be in touch." Hawke hung up before Apirak could say anymore, his shoulders tight with warning. The DEA had had plenty of time to trace the call. They'd be here soon, and he had no intention of waiting around to greet them.

Hawke had been gone three hours twenty minutes and fifteen seconds. Sixteen. Seventeen.

"Just keep counting. That's doing a whole lot of good." Miranda muttered the words out loud as she raked a hand through damp hair. In the time Hawke had been gone, she'd managed to go through every dresser drawer, the entire contents of the closet—where she found a T-shirt that fell to her thighs and jeans that perched precariously on her hips—take a shower, change clothes and scare herself silly. What she hadn't done was come up with a plan of action.

She rubbed at the ache behind her eyes and surveyed the items she'd collected. A pile of weapons lay on the bed—guns, knives and something she was sure was a machete. Wooden clubs attached by a short chain and another long wooden pole of some sort looked like martial arts weapons, though Miranda had no idea what they'd be used for. A box of ammunition was on the floor, deadly looking stuff that made her cringe. Beside it sat a small canister that she did recognize—pepper spray. At least she assumed it was pepper spray. She couldn't read the label. For all she knew it was something much more toxic. The sad fact was she had enough weapons to hold off an army, but she didn't know how to use most of them.

Who was she kidding? Even if she did know how to use them, she wasn't sure she'd be able to. Just the thought of shooting someone made her light-headed. Stabbing someone was even more appalling—the feel of a blade slicing through human flesh something she refused to even imagine.

She supposed she could try one of the more exotic-looking weapons. The chained wooden clubs seemed promising. She'd knocked Liam out and he'd survived. She could do the same to anyone who broke in. All she had to do was swing the clubs around a few times.

And brandish them uselessly while the enemy closed in.

"Face it. You're hopelessly ill prepared for this kind of thing." Miranda paced to the bedroom door, thought about opening it and changed her mind. Somehow having it closed and locked made her feel marginally safer. Which wasn't nearly safe enough. She imagined someone breaking down the door, rushing toward the room where she was hiding. Worse, imagined Hawke bloodied and dying, unable to return. Unable to ask for help.

"What am I supposed to do? Wait all day? All night? Wait a week?" The words were a prayer, one she could only hope God would answer in a way that she could understand rather than in the puzzling bits and pieces He most often seemed to use.

A stab of guilt went through her at the thought. The puzzles were hers, not God's. Even when the answers seemed clear, Miranda tended to doubt them. She'd spent five months deciding to break up with her high school boyfriend even though every one of her friends had been worried and was urging her to do so. Two years later, a year after becoming a Christian, she'd dated a man she'd met at the college bookstore. For six months she'd wondered at the strange feeling she had that the relationship wasn't what it seemed. It had taken running into Stan and his wife to show Miranda just how wrong the relationship was.

She'd even hesitated when it came to taking on responsibility for Justin, sure that she should finish her education first. Over and over again, God had brought people into her life, men and women with autistic children. Yet Miranda had refused to see them for what they were—clear direction and assurance that the course she was hesitating to take was the right one.

Only when Lauren had asked her to visit a facility where she planned to enroll Justin, did Miranda finally commit to God's plan. It had almost been too late, the paperwork all but signed.

Miranda didn't want to make the same mistake again. This time she wanted things to be different, wanted to listen to the soundless voice that spoke to her soul.

And right now, it was saying stay. Give Hawke more time. Trust that he'd return. More, trust that God was with her. That *He* was in control.

"Okay." Miranda whispered the words as she shoved aside the weapons she'd spread out on the bed and flopped down on the comforter. Her muscles were tight, her mind still racing, but she forced back the panic and listened to the silence. Deep. Placid. Devoid of danger.

For now she was safe.

That would just have to be enough.

TEN

"I've got it." David Sanchat shoved back from his desk and stood, his sallow skin pale, his dark eyes meeting Hawke's then shooting away. It hadn't been hard to find the man—Hawke had been keeping tabs on him for years and knew he'd taken a job as a professor at a university, knew he'd moved into a suburb just outside of Bangkok. It had been even less difficult to convince Sanchat to help. Having information that could destroy a man tended to make him very cooperative.

And the cooperation of a computer genius was exactly what Hawke needed.

He strode over to the computer screen, read the list of agents and the information about their locations. It was what he'd been hoping for—Jack McKenzie's address there for the taking. "Print it out for me."

"You know they're going to trace this back to me, right? A guy can't hack into the DEA's mainframe without getting caught." David's voice shook, his forehead beaded with sweat.

"That's not my problem."

"I could lose my job."

"Still not my problem."

"You're a cold son of—"

"And you paid for your party years acting as a courier for the Wa. Which do you think is worse?"

"What I did twelve years ago shouldn't matter. I'm a professor. A family man. A good citizen. And have been for a long time."

"The past can't be changed. The good we do can never pay for the sins we've committed. I think you know that." Hawke grabbed the printout from David's hand.

"This isn't about what I know or don't know. It's about you taking the law into your own hands. If the law wanted me, I would have been in jail a long time ago."

"I'm not taking the law into my own hands. I'm just helping it along. I believe in justice and that we all pay for our crimes eventually. This is your time to pay."

"Justice would mean *both* of us going to jail for the rest of our lives. Hacking into a U.S. government computer system—"

"You hacked into something that's open to DEA employees. Just a directory of names and contact information. Nothing top secret."

"That won't matter to the DEA. I'll lose everything for this." David collapsed into his computer chair, leaned his head against his hands. "Don't you think I regret what I did? I was young and stupid. My father was a diplomat. I traveled all over the world with him. Passing information from one place to another seemed like an easy way to make a few bucks."

"Your morality came too late for some. People die every day from drug overdoses or at the hands of the men who paid you."

"If I could change what I did, I would. I can't, so all that's left is to live the best life I can now." The words were spoken quietly and Hawke believed them. As much as he despised what Sanchat had done, he knew Sanchat's involvement with the Wa had ended years ago. Since then, the college professor had stayed out of trouble, devoting himself to his job and his family.

"When they come to question you, tell them I forced you to do this for me. Whatever else you choose to tell them is for you to decide."

"Listen, do you need anything else? Money? A ride?"

The questions caught Hawke by surprise and he hesitated with his hand on the office door. "Aren't you already in enough trouble?"

"Yeah, so I guess a little more isn't going to hurt."

"In for a penny, in for a pound?"

"Something like that."

"I've got everything I need."

"There'll be security guards near the front entrance of the building. You'll be better off going up to the roof and down the fire escape."

Hawke nodded and stepped out into the corridor, the quiet university closing in around him as he moved toward the stairwell, the need to hurry thrumming through him. He'd been away from the apartment for six hours. The time it had taken for Sanchat to access the DEA directory would only be worth it if Miranda was still waiting for him when he returned. He hoped she was. Sticking around Bangkok wasn't part of his plan. Neither was losing the woman who'd saved his life. If push came to shove, he'd comb the city until he found Miranda, but every minute he spent doing that was a minute his brother was in the enemy's hands.

It took only minutes to access the roof and descend to the street below. He moved along the sidewalk with purpose, but didn't rush, not wanting to call attention to himself. Bangkok never slept and the sounds of its nightlife drifted on humid night air, a pulsing beat that Hawke was all too familiar with. In years past, he'd traveled Bangkok's underworld, searching out those dealing in drugs and human flesh. Much of the money that passed hands there eventually made its way into the Wa's coffers. One name, one location, one exchange of money for drugs at a time, Hawke had provided information to the authorities that had chopped off the Wa's tail time and time again. The problem was, like many cold-blooded lizards, the Wa's tail just kept growing back.

And eventually Hawke realized that he was banging his head against a brick wall, that revenge would never be his for the taking, that justice would be meted out, just not by his hands or his power, that he was wasting his time, wasting his life on a futile effort that might lead his brother into the same cesspool of human depravity Hawke had been wading through.

He'd hoped living outside of Thailand would open doors to something different. That perhaps breaking his ties with his mother country was what was needed to end the journey he'd started after his family's murder. He'd wanted a new life. New goals. A fresh start.

Now, all he wanted was to find his brother and clear his name.

And keep Miranda safe.

An image flashed through his mind—dark hair, pale skin, freckles. Eyes the deep green of spring, new life and promises. As much as Hawke might be due to pay for some of the wrong he'd done, Miranda deserved to be home safe. He had every intention of getting her there.

The apartment building was straight ahead, a few windows illuminated. Most dark. Hawke entered silently, climbing the stairs two at a time, a sense of urgency spurring him on.

The apartment door was closed and locked, the lights in each room turned off. Hawke strode down the hall, scanning the floor for signs of light spilling from beneath the bedroom door. There were none. He used his key to unlock the door, pulling it open as he formulated a plan to find Miranda if she'd left.

He stepped into the room, flicked on the light, and froze, his mouth curving as he caught sight of the woman who'd been so much on his mind the last few hours. She lay sleeping, hair curling wildly around her face, her body drowning in a black T-shirt and baggy cargo-style jeans. Weapons were piled on the bed around her—knives, the unloaded guns he kept in the closet, pepper spray, ammo. A nunchaku was clutched in her hand as if she'd thought holding it while she slept would keep danger at bay.

Hawke strode across the room, touched her shoulder. "Miranda?"

She came up fast, the nunchaku still in her hand, her pulse beating wildly in the hollow of her throat. "You're back."

"Did you think I wouldn't return?"

"I was beginning to wonder." Her cheeks were pink from sleep, her eyes misty green. The circles under them looked darker than when Hawke had left, as if sleep had only made her more tired.

He brushed a lock of hair from her cheek, felt the silky softness of it. "I told you I'd be back."

"Yeah, I just wasn't sure I believed you." Her lips curved, but there was no smile in her eyes.

"You can always believe me, babe." He pulled the nunchaku from her hands, his tense muscles relaxing for the first time in hours. "Were you planning to use this as a weapon?"

"Only if I needed to."

"The gun might have been a better idea."

"I don't know how to use one." To Hawke's surprise, her voice broke on the words and she turned away, her shoulders stiff, something broken and lonely in her stance.

He reached for her hand, tugging her back toward him and wrapping his arms around her waist. "Are you okay?"

"I've been scared to death."

"You were safe here." He stroked her back, inhaling the sent of shampoo and soap. She'd taken a shower, but apples and cinnamon still seemed to hover in the air around her. Memory or reality, Hawke didn't know.

Her hands trembled as she slipped them under his pack and leaned back to look into his face. "I know. It was *you* I was scared for."

The sincerity in her eyes, the worry there, melted into Hawke's heart, touching something he hadn't allowed anyone near for a very long time.

He knew he should step back, put distance between them, but found himself pulling her closer instead. She fit perfectly, her head just under his chin, her hair soft against the skin of his throat. He wanted to stay there forever, absorbing the sweet artlessness of her embrace.

But they didn't have forever. Just moments, ticking by one after another while his brother remained in the hands of men who would stop at nothing to achieve their goals.

He loosened his hold, his hands lingering at the small of Miranda's back. "You didn't need to worry about me. I've been taking care of myself for a long time."

She shrugged, her hands fisted in his shirt, her knuckles warm through the material. "I'll try to remember that next time."

He wanted to tell her there wouldn't be a next time, but couldn't. They had a long journey ahead of them. Ten hours to Chiang Mai. Then on from there to Mae Hong Son. Anything could happen and probably would. His arms tightened around Miranda for a fraction of a second before he forced himself to step back. "We need to get moving. We've got a long way to go tonight."

"Where are we headed?" She stared up into his eyes, searching for something Hawke doubted she'd find. Honor, trustworthiness. Things he'd never been able to find in himself. At least not in the past ten years.

"Chiang Mai."

"I've never heard of it."

"It's north of here. About ten hours by road. " He grabbed a machete from the bed, picked up a can of pepper spray. Anything to keep his hands busy, his mind off what it felt like to hold Miranda in his arms—as if she belonged there, as if they'd been together a lifetime rather than a few short days.

She picked up the Uzi Hawke had confiscated from a drug runner across the border in Myanmar, holding it gingerly as if afraid it might go off in her hands.

"It's not loaded, babe."

"I wasn't sure. I don't have much experience with weapons. All I know is that you have a lot of them."

"I've collected them from some men who didn't need them anymore."

"That sounds….sinister."

"Most of them went to jail. Drug runners. Couriers. Men and women determined to spread the drug trade to every neighborhood and community in the world."

"That's what you do, then? Go after drug dealers?"

"What I do is run an export company in Bangkok. It's a family business. One my brother and I inherited after my father died. We buy handcrafted goods from the hill tribes up north and send them all over the world."

"Then how—"

"The story about how the rest of this came about is too long to tell now."

She opened her mouth, shut it again and shook her head. "Okay. I won't ask. It's none of my business anyway. Let's go."

She started away, but Hawke grabbed her arm, tugging her back around to face him. "I never said it wasn't your business. You deserve answers. I just can't give them now. We've got a long way to go and we've got a lot of people who'd like to stop us before we get there."

"That's an easy excuse, Hawke. I've been pulled into a situation I didn't ask to be in. I don't understand half of what or who is involved. I don't like not being in control. I don't like not having my life in my own hands."

"And I don't like talking about my past. It's not

something that's easy to share." He bit out the words, not wanting to give her even that, but knowing she deserved at least some of the truth.

"I guess that's something I *do* understand."

With that, she strode from the room. This time, Hawke let her go. There was nothing he could say, nothing he *should* say. Despite the heartache she'd suffered, Miranda had spent her life cut off from the uglier side of humanity. She didn't understand the darkness that Hawke walked through every day.

Or maybe she did. One way or another, he didn't want to taint her with the shadows that lived in his soul. That meant keeping his distance and that's exactly what he intended to do.

He put away the last of the weapons, grabbed more money from the safe in the closet, then left the room, closing and locking it behind him.

Miranda was waiting by the front door to the apartment, looking more like a child playing dress up than a grown woman. The hem of the T-shirt she'd borrowed fell to her thighs and the cuffs of the jeans bagged around her ankles. The whole outfit was way too long and cumbersome for the journey, but there was nothing Hawke could do about it now.

"Ready?"

"As I'll ever be. What will we do once we get to Chiang Mai?" Her eyes had flecks of gold and brown and seemed to change color as her emotion changed. First mossy green with fatigue. Then bright green with frustration. Now hazel with uncertainty.

"Have a little talk with my boss. First, though, we've got to get some food and a ride."

"I'm not hungry. Let's just go."

"Hungry or not, you need to eat." He pulled off his pack, grabbing fruit that he'd purchased from a vendor several hours before. "I've got bananas and rambutan. Which do you want?"

"I've only ever heard of the first, so I guess I'll have that."

"Live a little. Try something new." He peeled the round, spiny red fruit as they walked down stairs to the second floor, handing her the slick white meat inside.

Miranda took the fruit Hawke offered her, the slippery flesh silky in her hands. It had the sweetness of a grape and a texture slightly thicker than one. Her stomach rumbled in thanksgiving as she took another bite. "It's good."

"I thought you'd like it. Eat another." Hawke handed her a second peeled fruit, then used a key to unlock the door at the second floor landing, grabbing her hand and pulling her inside.

Unlike the rest of the building, this area was well kept, the walls freshly painted, the carpet thick and new looking. A garlicky aroma filled the air, making Miranda's already rumbling stomach growl in acknowledgment.

She pressed a hand against the sudden, gnawing ache of hunger and hurried behind Hawke. He bypassed the first and second apartment doors, rapping hard on the third. It opened immediately, a small, wizened man staring out at them.

"*Sawatdee khrap. Sabaaidee rue khrap?*" His raspy words were accompanied by a wide grin.

"*Koon Aran, Sawatdee khrap.*" Hawke spoke quietly, his tone fluid and musical, his hand still wrapped around Miranda's. She had the urge to lean her head against his shoulder and close her eyes for just a moment. She'd been sick with worry and fear for hours. Now, with Hawke back, his words flowing in a gentle cadence around her, she wanted to cave in, close off and forget for just a while the trouble she was in.

"Whoa! You're fading, babe." Hawke dragged her up against his side, his gaze smoky with concern and some other emotion Miranda couldn't name.

The older man looked alarmed and shouted something into the apartment before hurrying inside.

"I'm okay. Just daydreaming. What's going on?"

"*Koon* Aran has agreed to let us rent his motorcycle for a few days. He's gone to get it."

"From inside his apartment?"

"The people who live here have very little. What they have they can't afford to lose." As he spoke an elderly woman appeared carrying two bowls, a white porcelain spoon sticking up from each.

She spoke quietly, handing one bowl to Hawke and placing the other in Miranda's hands.

"She says to eat."

"What is it?" Miranda glanced down into the bowl, the scent of spring onions wafting from the steamy contents. Wide noodles, small chunks of meat and bits of onion floated in light brown broth.

"*Lat Na*. Rice noodles in broth with chicken." Hawke didn't waste any time digging in to his, and Miranda realized he must be as hungry as she was. Had he eaten while he was gone? Or had he gone hungry the way Miranda had?

He lifted a brow, gestured toward her bowl of noodles. "Eat."

She did as he suggested, the warmth of the soup

sliding straight into her energy-starved body. "It's good."

"New things aren't always bad." His lips curved, his hard features softening.

Despite her anxiety, Miranda's own lips curved in response. She might still be in danger, might still be running for her life, but at least she wasn't alone. The relief of having Hawke back with her would have been comforting if she weren't so sure that what was coming next was going to be worse than what she'd already experienced. "I still think I'd rather be home."

"You will be."

"When?"

"Soon."

Miranda might have asked exactly what he meant by soon, but the elderly man appeared in the threshold of the door, a black motorcycle rolling along beside him.

Hawke pulled a wad of cash from his pocket, handed it and their empty bowls over. Then he turned and met Miranda's gaze. "Ready?"

No, but the only other choice was to stay behind and there was no way Miranda was going to do that. "Yes. Let's go."

He grabbed her hand again, his fingers curving around hers, his calloused palm rasping against her skin. She shivered at the contact, the warmth that spread through her at Hawke's touch something she hadn't expected and didn't want.

"Cold?" His words whispered against her ear and she shook her head, afraid if she spoke he'd hear what she was feeling.

"All right then. Let's go." He squeezed her hand then let it go, rolling the bike down the hall.

Miranda hurried after him. In just a few minutes they'd be on the way to Chiang Mai, heading toward the answers they needed so desperately. Miranda wanted to believe they'd find them, that Hawke had been right when he'd said she'd be home soon. But something told her that her journey through Thailand had just begun and that things would get much worse before they got better.

If they got better.

As she stepped out into the balmy night, she could only pray that they would.

ELEVEN

Miranda had ridden on the back of a motorcycle before, but never on a dark, empty road in a foreign land; never when she was running from the police and being chased by a killer. Helmetless, she clung to Hawke's back as the bright lights of the city faded into the distance and the heavily populated suburbs gave way to open, empty land. Rain was in the air. She could feel it in the moisture that clung to her skin and turned her wild, whipping hair into a sodden, slapping mass of curls. Soon the sky would open up, pouring gallons of rain down on their heads, but even then they couldn't afford to stop. There was too much at stake. Their lives. Their freedom. The life of Hawke's brother. She knew it. Hawke knew it. No discussion was needed on the subject. They'd drive until they needed gas. Then they'd drive some more.

Mile after mile, minute after minute passed, the first sixty not bad, the second more uncomfortable. By the third, Miranda was shivering with cold, the thin cotton T-shirt she wore no buffer against the chilly night air. The scent of wet earth, rotting plants and asphalt filled her lungs and clogged her throat. She coughed, but couldn't dislodge the moist fetid air.

"You okay?" Hawke shouted the words above the roar of the engine, his words breaking the monotony of the ride for the first time since they'd left Bangkok.

"Yes."

"You're shivering."

"It's a little cold, but I'll be fine."

To her surprise, the bike slowed, easing to the side of the road, and then stopping, the engine dying, the sudden silence deafening.

Hawke shifted, his shadowy form angling toward her. "A little cold? You're shaking like a leaf."

He rubbed her arms, his hands sliding against cotton and flesh, generating heat Miranda desperately needed.

"Better?"

"Yes."

"Hop off the bike." Miranda did as he suggested, watching as Hawke did the same. He pulled off his jacket, wrapped it around her shoulders. "Put that on."

"You need it more than I do. I've at least got someone blocking the wind."

"Don't worry. Being prepared for trouble may not make life's journey less bumpy, but it makes those bumps more comfortable. Always be prepared."

"Another Hawke Morran quote?"

"A Patrick Morran quote. My stepfather loved to mix his own wisdom with that of history's great sages." He pulled off his pack, grabbed a lightweight jacket out of it, and shrugged it on.

"It sounds like he was a neat guy."

"He was. Why don't we stretch our legs? Have some water?"

"I've got another five hours in me before I need a good stretch." That wasn't quite the truth, but there was no way Miranda planned to be the reason they had to take a break.

"You're a trooper, babe." There was a smile in his voice. "But even the toughest soldier has to stop sometimes." He zipped the jacket she'd put on, and pulled the collar up around her neck, his scent enveloping her—masculine and strong.

"I may be tired of riding on the back of this motorcycle, but not tired enough to risk our lives or your brother's to take a break."

"Have you always been like this, Miranda Sheldon?" His hands framed her face, his eyes gleaming in the darkness.

Miranda's face heated beneath his touch, her mind suddenly blank. "Like what?"

"Practical. Determined."

"No." She use to be a dreamer, her head filled with fairy tales, but that had changed. One too many broken promises. One too many shattered dreams. "I've had to learn to be. My nephew was autistic. Practicality and determination went a long way in creating a good life for Justin."

"And love. I bet you showered your nephew with love." His hands slipped from her face, and he tugged her a few steps away from the motorcycle, darkness pressing in around them. Somehow it freed the words that Miranda hadn't been able to say. Not to Lauren. Not to Max. Not to friends. Barely to herself. "Yes, but in the end, I failed him. The night he died, I was going to a bridal shower, leaving him with my sister for the night."

"Leaving him with his mother."

"*I* was his mother. I should never have left them

together. Lauren is self-absorbed. She couldn't be expected to care for someone with Justin's needs."

"What happened?"

"Justin wandered outside while Lauren was on the phone. He was hit by a drunk driver just a block from our house. I know he was looking for me." Her voice broke, and she stopped, tears clogging her throat and seeping from her eyes.

"You can't know that." Hawke wrapped his arms around her, pulling Miranda's head to his chest, his hand stroking her hair.

"Maybe not, but I believe it." She let herself relax, the beat of his heart, the quiet inhalations of his breathing steady and sure and as familiar as her own. How that could be, she didn't know. They were different in every way, his past so far removed from her's that they were like creatures from different planets. She was quiet, bookish, boring. He was energy, action, barely concealed violence. Yet she couldn't deny the thread that stretched between them, pulling them closer with every moment spent together.

The thought made her uncomfortable and she stepped out of his embrace. "We need to get going again."

"We do, but not before I tell you this." He shifted, leaning close and staring into her eyes. His face was a stone sculpture, cold and hard with only a hint of human warmth beneath it. "I've learned in life, babe, that we can't change yesterday. Believing you could have done something to prevent your nephew's death is a waste of energy. Instead, you should remember all the love you gave him while he was alive and know you did the best you could for him."

"That isn't easy to do."

"No, but in the end it's the only way we can keep from being destroyed." He sounded like he knew what he was talking about and Miranda strained to see more of his expression in the dim light. All she saw were hard angles, harsh planes and secrets; the kind of man that, if she saw him on the street she'd avoid. Yet, here they were a team. Together for however long it took to find the person who'd set Hawke up. Maybe coincidence had brought them together. Or maybe God had. If so, there was a reason for it. One Miranda could only hope she'd eventually understand.

"Hawke—"

"You were right, we do need to go." He led her back to the motorcycle and climbed on, his tense muscles telling her more than words just how closed the conversation was.

It was for the best. Building more of a connection with Hawke could only be a mistake. Once this was over, he'd go his way. She'd go hers. It was as inevitable as getting back on the motorcycle and heading toward whatever trouble awaited them in Chiang Mai.

Miranda sighed, climbing on the bike behind Hawke, wrapping her arms around his waist, her eyes trained on the asphalt stretching out before them, beckoning them to answers or to death. Miranda shuddered and for just a moment Hawke's hand covered hers, his fingers pressing gently in silent support.

And the thread that stretched between them wound itself just a little tighter around her heart.

Golden fingers crept across the horizon as Hawke pulled the motorcycle into an alley and parked it. The buildings on either side were three stories high, their whitewashed brick facades stark in the hazy purplish light. Cars and motorcycles zipped past the mouth of the alley, rickety pickup trucks and rumbling buses interspersed between them. The humid air was thick with the scent of garlic, spices and a sweet flowery scent that Miranda didn't recognize.

This was Chiang Mai.

Miranda didn't know if she should be relieved that they'd finally arrived at their destination or terrified of what would come next.

Hawke climbed off the bike and offered a hand to Miranda. If he was tired, it didn't show. There were no shadows beneath his eyes, no hollowness to his face. Black stubble covered his jaw and his eyes were eerily light against his tan skin. "That last hour was rough. You did good, babe."

"All I did was hold on."

"That's a whole lot better than the alternative." He smiled, extending a hand and pulling Miranda off the motorcycle. "Unfortunately, we're not done yet. We've got three blocks to go before we're where we need to be."

"Your boss's house?"

"Yes. He lives in a compound in town. It shouldn't be hard to get there. Provided he doesn't already know we're coming."

His words did what arriving in Chiang Mai hadn't, shooting adrenaline into Miranda's blood and giving her the energy she needed to move. "And if he does?"

"Then we'll know it soon enough. Come on." He led her to the mouth of the alley and onto a street alive with early-morning traffic. A vendor moved up the sidewalk pushing a silver cart, a wide-brimmed straw hat hiding his face, his flip-flops slapping against the concrete as he walked. A woman swept the pavement in front of a store, the fan-shape broom swooshing with each brush and sway. It seemed a peaceful, ordinary morning, but that didn't mean trouble wasn't lurking around the next corner.

"Do you think they're out here looking for us?" She whispered the question, afraid that speaking too loudly would upset the balance and send the world tumbling back into terror.

"The DEA or friends of the man who set me up?"

"Either. Both."

"There's a chance, but I'm banking on them heading to Mae Hong Son instead."

"What's in Mae Hong Son?"

"I have a home there. Men who work for me. Resources available to me. It would make sense for me to go there." He pulled her around a corner and down a side street, his stride long and confident, as if he had no fear at all that they'd be spotted.

"What do you plan to do when we get to your boss's house?" *If* they got there. Miranda still wasn't sure they would.

"Nothing much. I just want to have a little chat with him." The grim tone warned Miranda that there might be a lot more to Hawke's plan than he was letting on.

"What if *he* doesn't want to have a chat with *you?*"

"Did I say I was going to give him a choice?" Hawke shot a look in her direction, his eyes steel-gray and cold.

"Not unless I have to."

"I don't like the sound of that." Miranda grabbed the

sleeve of Hawke's jacket and stopped. "If you do something to him, we'll be in even more trouble than we're already in."

"Babe, we can't possibly be in any more trouble. Besides, Jack McKenzie and I have known each other for years. He'll tell me what I want to know."

"I don't know about this."

"I do."

"Wouldn't it be better if you called your boss instead? Just asked him the questions over the phone."

"It would be better if you were quiet for a while. This isn't a touristy part of town and your English is going to call attention to us."

"Sorry."

"Don't be sorry, babe. Just be quiet." He grinned and squeezed her hand.

Miranda's heart skipped a beat, but she couldn't quite return the smile. For all Hawke knew, there were a hundred men waiting for them at his boss's house, ready to arrest them. Or kill them.

"We're here," Hawke whispered close to her ear, his words barely vibrating in the air.

Here was a thick white wall topped with shards of glass that glistened in the early-morning sun. Blades of yellow grass clung to the base of the wall, scraggly and unsure.

"Ever ride a horse?"

Hawke's question took Miranda by surprise and for a moment she could think of no answer. Finally, she nodded. "A few times."

"Good. Hand me the jacket."

Miranda shrugged out of Hawke's jacket and passed it to him, watching with growing worry as he tossed it onto the top of the fence. Surely he didn't plan for them to scale the fence. If he did, he was going to be disappointed in Miranda's climbing abilities. She'd spent her childhood reading books, not climbing trees and jumping fences.

"You first. I'll follow." Hawke gestured to the wall, and Miranda took a step back.

"I'm not very good at this sort of thing."

"Sure you are. I'll give you a leg up. Just mount the fence like you would a horse. Then lower yourself down the other side."

"There isn't a horse alive as tall as that fence. It must be ten feet high."

"Eight." His eyes dared her as he cupped his hands together and waited.

She took a deep breath, nodded her head. "All right, let's do it."

Hawke smiled again, a crooked grin that hooked Miranda's heart and tugged hard. She looked away, not wanting him to see the heat staining her cheeks; not wanting to contemplate the reasons *why* heat was staining her cheeks.

If Hawke noticed her discomfort, he didn't comment. Instead, he grabbed her foot, supporting the arch in his hands. "Make sure you go over the jacket. The glass shards will tear your hands to pieces if you don't."

Miranda nodded, though torn hands were the least of her worries. If she wasn't careful, she'd go over on her head and break her neck. She just prayed she'd manage to land on her feet.

Hawke straightened, boosting Miranda in a quick, effortless movement that had her sailing upward at an alarming rate. She grabbed the top of the fence, spiky glass digging into her skin despite the thick leather of the jacket. A quick pivot, a swing of her leg and she was over, dangling by her hands, her feet scratching against stucco as she tried to convince herself to drop.

A thump and bang warned her that Hawke was on his way over, but still she couldn't release her grip.

"Are you planning to hang there all day?" Hawke's gruff voice whispered down at her. She looked up, saw him perched on the fence, balancing on the balls of his feet and looking completely at ease.

"Is there anything you can't do?" She panted the words out, her arms burning from the effort it took to hold her weight.

"I can't jump eight feet to the ground and I can't drop from this spot until you do."

He had a point. Even if he hadn't, Miranda's fingers were slipping from the leather. She closed her eyes, released her hold and dropped, tumbling onto her backside in the fragrant grass and moist earth.

Seconds later, Hawke landed next to her, dropping down in a crouch, his eyes searching her face.

"Good job, babe. You okay?" His lips touched her ear as he spoke, the warmth of it shivering along her nerves.

"Right as rain." Even if she was trembling from head to toe. She hadn't broken her neck and that was definitely something to be thankful for.

Hawke stared her down for a moment, then stood, pulling her to her feet. "Good. Come on. McKenzie's house is number 1492."

"What if he's not home?"

"Then we go in and take a look around."

"That's illegal."

"So is selling information to drug dealers. So is murder."

"Do you really think he's responsible?"

"I don't know, but I plan to find out."

"Hawke—"

"You need to stop worrying so much. It's bad for your health."

"So is stress and I've been under a tremendous amount of that ever since I met you."

"Then we'll have to make sure to do something relaxing and fun when this is over." He didn't say *if* it was over, but Miranda was thinking it as Hawke tugged her to the edge of a stucco-sided house. "Here's what I want you to do. Walk around to the front of this house and take a look at the number."

"Me?"

"I'd do it, but you're much more innocuous looking."

He was right, and Miranda wasn't even going to try to convince him otherwise. No one would look at her and see a threat. Hawke, on the other hand, was six foot two of pure trouble.

She took a deep breath, prayed she wouldn't be spotted and stepped around the side of the house.

TWELVE

Early morning light washed the world in dull color as Miranda moved across the front yard, the flowers, trees and buildings taking on a sepia tone. Sodden grass squished beneath her feet, the scent of wet earth pungent and full. The community lay silent and sleeping, doors closed, shades drawn, unsuspecting, unaware. All Miranda had to do was get the house number and get back to Hawke's side. Easy.

Except she couldn't see a house number. Not on the door. Not on the mailbox. Not anywhere obvious.

"It's got to be somewhere." She muttered the words, her heart pumping so fast and so loud, she was sure it would wake the entire neighborhood.

"Can I help you, miss?" a deep voice called from somewhere behind her, and Miranda spun to face the speaker, hoping she didn't look as terrified as she felt.

The man was tall, skinny and wearing a crisp brown uniform, a hat and a belt with a radio and some kind of club hanging from it. A guard. Miranda's blood froze in her veins, her mind blank. Every word, every thought jumbled in her head, refusing to coalesce into coherent words.

"Miss?" He stepped closer, his smile turning to a frown, his hand dropping to the radio he carried. "Is everything okay?

"Everything is fine. I'm just out for a walk. It's such a beautiful morning." If her smile looked as forced as it felt the dark-eyed, clean-shaven young man would know in an instant that something was wrong. She needed to relax, pretend she belonged.

But she didn't belong and she couldn't relax and she *still* didn't know what to say.

"You are a friend of *Koon* Miller?" He motioned toward the house, the sharp edge to his gaze a warning that things might be about to go very badly.

Miranda scrambled for an answer. Yes was what her head insisted she say. No was what her gut wanted her to respond. "No. I'm a friend of…" What had Hawke said his boss's name was? "Mr. McKenzie. I couldn't sleep, so I thought I'd go for a walk, but now I'm turned around and can't seem to find his house. They all look the same." And they did—white stucco, orange shutters, wide driveways and manicured lawns.

The guard seemed to relax at her words and he smiled. "Ah. I see. You came last night in the van?"

"No, yesterday afternoon. I'm in from the States." *Please let that be the right answer.*

The young man nodded. "It's easy to get confused when you first arrive. *Koon* McKenzie's house is just five houses up on this side of the street." He gestured to the left. "You will be staying a while?"

"Yes."

"Good. There's much to see here. You've been to Thailand before?"

"No, this is my first trip." Miranda wanted desperately to make an excuse and hurry away, but didn't dare.

"Go see the elephants then. All visitors like the elephants."

"I will." *Pretend you have all day. Pretend you have nothing to hide.* The words chanted through her mind, her heart pounding so hard and fast, she thought it would explode from her chest.

"Good. My shift is ending. If you go for a walk tomorrow morning, look for me. I'm Klahan."

"M— Margaret."

He smiled again, flashing white teeth and offering a bow. Miranda followed his example, then waved as the guard walked away, her heart still slamming against her ribs, her pulse racing.

She needed to find Hawke and get out fast, but forced herself to walk toward McKenzie's house until the guard disappeared around the corner. Only then did she do what she so desperately wanted to—racing through a side yard, heading back toward the fence. Her feet slipped in wet grass and mud and she flew backward, her arms scrambling for purchase. Hard hands wrapped around her waist, pulling her upright and preventing her from taking a seat on the grass again.

Hawke.

Miranda knew it even before he whispered in her ear. "This is becoming a habit."

"Me falling, you helping me or me getting us into trouble?" she whispered back, her shaky words sounding louder than she intended.

"You forgot one—you getting us *out* of trouble. I thought I might have to come take care of things, but you handled the situation well."

"Don't be too sure of that. I think we need to get out of here while we still can." She started toward the fence, but Hawke pulled her up short.

"We can't leave until McKenzie and I have a little talk. Besides, the guard bought your story. You even managed to get the location of McKenzie's house out of him."

"Hawke, I really think we should leave."

"We've got no choice but to stick it out. McKenzie is either guilty, or has some idea of who is. He can give us the name and location of the people who knew I was in the States. Without those, we may as well head back to Maryland and turn ourselves in."

Miranda wasn't sure that was a bad idea, but as much as she'd like to believe going home was the answer, she knew they'd face just as much danger there. Maybe more. Once in police custody, they'd have no way of defending themselves against whatever threat Green and his men offered.

She kept her mouth shut and followed Hawke through one backyard after another. His footsteps were silent, his movements lithe and fluid. He barely seemed to disturb the air. Miranda, on the other hand, stepped on every stick and every loose stone, brushed against bushes and low-hanging leaves, and made enough noise to alert anyone who might be listening that she was trespassing. The way she saw it, if their success was based on the ability to reach McKenzie's house silently, she was blowing their chances big-time.

"This is it." Hawke paused at the corner of a house that looked like every other house in the community.

"You're sure this is the fifth house?"

"Positive."

"What now?"

He gestured toward the back door. "See the shoes?"

She did. Yellow flip-flops sat neatly on a cement slab outside the closed back door. "Yes."

"They're not McKenzie's. They're his maid's."

"Which means?"

"Maids in communities like this visit each other for coffee or tea in the morning before their employers wake up. They always use the back door. All we have to do is knock and wait. We'll be in before McKenzie gets out of bed."

"Are you crazy? We can't just knock on the door and then push our way in." She grabbed Hawke's arm, but he kept moving toward the door, Miranda's dragging heels not slowing him in the least.

"Sure we can. It might not be the best plan, but it's the only one we've got. And—" he paused, patting his side and the gun that was strapped there "—if it doesn't work, I've got backup."

"What if the maid doesn't open the door?"

"She'll open the door."

"What if—"

He knocked. Two soft raps on the door, as if he knew exactly how a maid might gain her friend's attention. He must have. The door opened, a woman's voice audible before the interior of the room was visible. It halted abruptly, a small dark-haired woman, standing in the threshold, her mouth open, her eyes wide.

Hawke moved past her, speaking in Thai, the gun suddenly in his hand.

"Hawke—"

"She knows I'm not going to hurt her. She just needs

to cooperate." He said something else in Thai, his gentle tone contrasting sharply with the gun he still held.

The woman nodded, speaking quickly and gesturing toward a doorway that led farther into the house.

"What's she saying?" Miranda's heart slammed against her ribs, her stomach knotted with anxiety. They shouldn't be here. They should have turned themselves in, not come halfway around the world for answers.

"McKenzie is home. Stay here and make sure the maid doesn't leave. I'm going to find him."

Arguing would only waste time and Miranda was desperate to be done and gone. She nodded, trying to smile at the Thai woman, but only managing a grimace.

"I won't be long." Hawke spoke as he stepped out of the room and disappeared from sight.

Miranda stood in taut silence, her ears straining to hear evidence that Hawke had found McKenzie, her gaze on the maid who shuffled around the bright kitchen as if this were any other day, as if a man with a gun hadn't just gone looking for her boss.

"You want tea?" The Thai woman gestured to a pot on the stove.

"No, thank you."

"Food?"

"No. I'm fine." Discussing food and drinks while Hawke was stalking through the house with a gun seemed bizarre, and Miranda wondered what Hawke had said to the woman that had her offering hospitality rather than hysteria.

"You sit down then."

A loud thud sounded from somewhere above their heads, the crash making both women jump. Another crash followed the first and Miranda grabbed the other woman's hand. "We've got to see what's going on."

"No. We stay here."

"We're going." She gritted her teeth and pulled the smaller woman across the room and through the doorway. Silence had returned and that worried Miranda more than the thud and crash she'd heard.

"Where is Mr. McKenzie?" She asked the question as she hurried across a long, white-walled living room.

"Upstairs getting ready for work. But we stay down here. We don't interrupt."

Miranda ignored the protest and started up the stairs, still clutching the maid's arm. If Hawke was in control of the situation, she'd go back down to the kitchen. If he wasn't...

What?

What could she possibly do? She didn't have a weapon, didn't have a plan. All she had was adrenaline speeding through her body and fear burning at the back of her throat. Maybe she could get her hands on the gun, or grab a vase or lamp from somewhere in the room. Though she doubted hitting McKenzie over the head with either would be an option. She'd need the element of surprise for that and between her huffing breaths and the maid's high-pitched protest, Miranda felt pretty sure she'd lost that.

The upstairs hallway was empty, three closed doors beckoning. "Which room is McKenzie's?"

Before the maid had a chance to reply, a scuffling sound carried from the room at the far end of the hall, the door banged open and a man stumbled out. Medium height and build with unremarkable features, dressed in a dark suit and understated tie, he looked about as dangerous as a butterfly.

Miranda stepped back anyway, her pulse racing as she searched the dark recesses beyond the door for Hawke. She didn't have long to wait. He moved into sight, his gun down by his side, a scowl darkening his face. "Didn't I tell you to wait downstairs?"

"I heard banging. I thought you might need help."

His scowl deepened, pulling at the corners of his mouth and creasing his forehead, his eyes the brooding gray of February sky. "Everything is under control. Jack was just telling me where my brother is."

"I was just telling you that your brother escaped while he was being transported to Bangkwang prison. If I knew where he was, he'd be back in custody." Jack McKenzie's voice was as unassuming as his face, his demeanor relaxed and unperturbed, as if he'd been expecting them and was glad they'd finally arrived.

Miranda edged back toward the staircase, sure she'd hear the sounds of slamming doors and pounding feet. If McKenzie had been expecting them, it was only a matter time before his backup arrived.

"Hawke, I think we should leave." Her voice sounded thick and rough, the taste of fear bitter on her tongue.

"Not until I get my answers." Hawke's gaze never left McKenzie.

"I've given you the only answer I have, Morran." McKenzie's gaze shifted to Miranda, his sharp focus disconcerting. "You must be Miranda Sheldon. A lot of people in the States are worried about you. I'm glad to see you're all right."

"I'd be better if you'd tell Hawke what he wants to know, so we can leave and you can get on with your day."

"There's no need for you to rush away. We have plenty of time for discussion—my ride to work won't be here for another twenty minutes."

"Only if that discussion has to do with who set me up and what you're going to do about it." Hawke bit the words out.

"It will." Jack lips curved in a smile that didn't reach his eyes.

"You know something." Hawke shoved his gun into his shoulder holster and leaned against the doorframe. "Why don't you stop playing games and tell me what?"

"No games, Morran. I don't know where your brother is and I don't know who set you up, but I believe someone did. We've been this close to Green several times in the past few years. He always slips through our fingers. We've suspected for a while that someone has been leaking information to him. Now we know it for sure. There were only a few men who knew you were working for us. It has to be one of them."

"Or you."

"You don't think it's me anymore than I think you killed a man in cold blood to steal fifty thousand dollars. Though, I've got to admit, I'd have preferred it to be you rather than any of my men."

"Thanks."

Jack shrugged. "None of us want to believe someone we trust would betray us or the ideals and principles we represent. I'm sure you felt the same way when Sang Lao bought one of your people last year and that young girl was taken right out from under your nose."

Hawke's lips tightened, and he nodded. Obviously, he knew exactly what Jack was referring to.

Miranda wished she did. She'd thought Jack and Hawke would be adversaries, facing each other from opposite sides. Instead, it seemed they had some trust for one another. That could only be good. She prayed that Jack would tell them everything was okay, that the DEA knew Hawke was innocent and was working hard to find the guilty party, but as the two men stared tight-jawed at one another, she had the sinking feeling that wasn't going to happen.

Finally, Hawke spoke, not moving from his post by the door. Though he seemed relaxed, Miranda sensed his coiled tension. "What are your plans, McKenzie? Obviously you have one, or we wouldn't be standing here discussing things."

"I plan to fix some leaky plumbing and I think you're just the man to help me."

"I'm no plumber, McKenzie. All I want is my brother, and the proof I need to get back to my life."

"I'd say our goals are the same. We can accomplish more together than we can alone."

"And I'd say we had this conversation twelve months ago when you told me I was just the man to help you bring down Harold Green. All that's gotten me in a truckload of trouble. I'm thinking this time, I'll stick to helping myself."

"What about Miranda? If you go down. She goes down, too."

"I don't plan to go down." Hawke smiled, a feral showing of teeth that held no humor.

"But someone has to."

"Then let's play this my way. *You* help *me*. Then we'll talk about what I can do for you."

Miranda was sure that Jack would refuse, that he'd

tell Hawke that things were going to be done his way or no way at all. Instead, he nodded. "Fair enough. What do you need me to do?"

cut the mark. There were nuns during the day preparing to stay small and be quicker. He's right in position. What do you want to do?"

THIRTEEN

Hawke wasn't surprised that Jack agreed to his terms. Though they'd never actually worked together, the other man's reputation was well-known, his fierce commitment to putting a stop to the drugs being trafficked out of Thailand making him a formidable adversary to those who made money off illegal narcotics. As much as Hawke had suspected Jack of being the leak, he'd been relieved to find it wasn't true.

"I want the names of everyone who knew I was working for you."

"It's a short list. Five of us made the decision to bring you in on the Green case." Jack spouted off four names. None were familiar to Hawke, though that was about to change.

"Are you investigating any of them?"

"We've investigated everyone in the Chiang Mai office over the past year. There's nothing that indicates anyone has been taking payoffs. They're all living within their means, none have extra money in their bank accounts."

"That doesn't mean much."

"It means we don't have just cause to pull anyone in

for questioning. It also means you're the perfect scapegoat. You've skirted the law too many times, Hawke. It finally caught up with you. Our man knew he could warn Green of the sting we'd set up and throw you to the wolves afterward. He probably assumed there'd be no one willing to believe your story."

"He assumed I'd be too dead to tell it. I'll need names, addresses and work schedules for all four of those men."

"Breaking and entering is against the law."

"That's never stopped me before."

"You know that if you get caught I had nothing to do with this."

"And if I find the leak and the evidence we need to prove it?"

"Then we'll pretend the breaking and entering didn't happen and you can either go back to your life here or return to the States a free man." He flashed a cold, hard smile. "The way I see it, if someone in my office is leaking information to Green, it's a good possibility that person is in the Wa's pocket. Breaking a few laws is a small price to pay for finding out who it is."

"Maybe you and I are more alike than I thought."

"We're more alike than you could ever know." The words were grim, belying Jack's bland expression. He pulled a folded paper from his jacket pocket, handed it to Hawke. "I've written down names and addresses. All four men are working today."

"You're very prepared considering you didn't know I was coming."

"Who said I didn't know?" Jack drummed his fingers against his arms, his gaze conveying what Hawke had only begun to suspect.

"You had this all planned before I went to the States. This was your real goal." Anger reared up, hot and searing, but Hawke tamped it down. There would be time later to discuss McKenzie's methods.

"My goal was to take Green down. I'd be lying if I said I wasn't hoping we'd also find our leak."

"Didn't you care that you put Hawke in a dangerous situation? That he could have been killed?" Miranda spoke quietly, her eyes the color of mountains in the mist, jungle foliage, lush fields.

The color of home.

Hawke's heart clenched, closing against the thought and the longing that went with it. He'd given up the dream long ago, had accepted well before he'd met Miranda that there would never be soft arms and warm smiles to go home to.

"I've known Hawke for years, Ms. Sheldon. I had every confidence he could take care of himself." Jack's smooth baritone and ingratiating smile grated on Hawke's nerves, but it was the way the man's gaze traveled Miranda's body, touching on her face, lingering on her lips, that made him want to knock his head off.

He bit back the urge. Barely.

"Jack believes the end justifies the means."

"And you don't, Morran?"

Did he? A year ago, he would have readily agreed. But not anymore. He'd changed. Softened. Become more aware of something much deeper and truer than himself. Though if he were honest, he'd admit that the change had been taking place for much longer than a year. He'd been changing since the day Noah Stone had carried him half-dead from the jungle. Hawke wasn't sure he was happy about it and was even less sure there was anything he could do about it.

"One more thing." Jack spoke quietly, his gaze hard. "There's already a cell in the Bangkok Hilton with your name on it. I'm the only reason you're not in it yet. If I so much as *think* I made a mistake in trusting you, I'll pull you in so fast your head will spin. You'll spend the rest of your life rotting in Bangkwang prison and I won't feel one bit of guilt over it."

"And if I find out you really are the leak, you won't have to worry about spending time in Bangkwang."

"As long as we understand each other." Jack's shoulder's relaxed. "I think you should leave the woman with me."

"The *woman* isn't being left anywhere." Miranda stiffened, her gaze jumping from Jack to Hawke and back again.

"You've been through a lot this past week, Ms. Sheldon. Having all this happen on the heels of your nephew's death must have exhausted you." His words were warm as melted butter.

Hawke gritted his teeth to keep from saying something rude. It was no business of his if Jack wanted to play nice to a beautiful woman. Except that Miranda wasn't just any woman. She was Miranda. Hawke had to resist the desire to smash his fist into Jack's smiling face.

"I'm fine, Mr. McKenzie." Miranda didn't return Jack's smile. Her gaze was solemn. The new hollows beneath her cheekbones and the sprinkling of freckles against her ashen skin made Hawke want to pull her toward him, wrap an arm around her waist and stake a claim he had no right to.

"And I want you to stay that way." Jack pressed his point. "If you stay here, I can guarantee your safety."

"Like you guaranteed my brother's?" Hawke couldn't stop the sarcasm that seeped into his words anymore than he could have stopped the tide from rolling in.

"Everything that happened to your brother was outside my jurisdiction."

"That's bull. You sent men to question him. Your agency handed him over to the police."

"And that's where our responsibility for him ended. Beside, Ms. Sheldon is in a different situation. She's not going to be taken anywhere. She can stay here."

"While you're at work? Anything could happen."

"Why would it? No one knows she's here. Even if someone found out, there are guards stationed at the gate. They won't let anyone get in."

"They let us in." Miranda interrupted the argument, her words quiet, but firm.

"Ms. Sheldon, I don't think you understand how much danger Hawke will be in once he steps outside this complex."

"I don't think *you* understand how much danger we've already been in. Partly because of you." She sounded weary and Hawke decided it was time to end the argument.

"She's coming with me." He took Miranda's hand and started moving toward the steps, but Jack grabbed his arm.

"You can't do your job if you're worrying about her."

"Which is why I'm not leaving her here. I'll be in touch as soon as I know something." He turned his back on the other man, shrugging away from his hold.

Though Hawke knew he wanted to, Jack didn't argue

any further, just followed them down the stairs and to the back door. "I'm the second pickup of the day. The van starts at Laurence's apartment. You'll want to go there first."

"You going to tell anyone I was here?"

"The news will get out one way or another." Jack cut a look toward his maid who'd been listening wide-eyed for much too long. "It's best if it comes from me."

"What are you going to tell them?"

"That you came in with a gun, looking for information about your brother and claiming you were set up."

"The truth is always the best cover."

"You and I really are alike, Morran." Jack pulled the back door open. "Good luck and Godspeed."

"I'll need both."

"You'll find your quarry. You always do."

He was right and this time would be no different. Not with the stakes so high. Simon's life and Miranda's hung in the balance. Failing the mission would mean failing them. "If you hear any news of my brother, call my compound in Mai Hong Son. I'll check in there periodically."

"Will do."

Hawke felt Jack's hard stare as he and Miranda moved away from the house, but he didn't look back. There was a lot of ground to cover before this journey ended. Looking back would only slow things down.

"Where to now?" The weariness in Miranda's voice remained, the deep circles beneath her eyes speaking of sleepless nights and fear.

"I'm heading to an apartment complex a few miles from here. I'm thinking that maybe you *should* stay here." A few hours alone in Jack's house might be preferable to dragging an obviously exhausted woman through the streets of Chiang Mai.

She blinked, shook her head. "I don't agree."

"When have you ever?" He smiled, caressed the smooth skin of her hand. "You'll be safe here for a few hours and that's all the time this will take me. You can rest, get ready for whatever happens next."

"While you're off fighting bad guys? I don't think so." The worry in her voice, in her eyes would have been humorous if Hawke hadn't been so touched by it.

He'd learned to take care of himself early. The death of his biological father, a marine who'd served in Vietnam, forced his mother to take on long hours of work to support Hawke. By the time Patrick Morran came into the picture, Hawke was ten years old going on twenty—responsible, hardworking and determined. No one had felt the need to worry about him. Since his parent's death, few had bothered.

And now he was staring into the eyes of a woman who had every right to be worried about herself, every reason to be moaning at her fate.

Instead all her energy, all her worry seemed to be for him.

"You don't need to worry about me, babe." He held her chin in his hand, her skin soft and smooth beneath his palm. "I've been doing this sort of thing for a long time. I'll be fine."

"And I'll be with you to make sure you are."

"Miranda—"

"I'm safer with you than alone. You know it. So do I. If you leave me behind, I'll just come looking for you. Now, come on. We're wasting time. I want to get this done."

"If you come with me, you do what I say."

"I always do."

"I can name at least two times when you didn't. Both could have gotten you killed."

"I thought you needed my help."

"I didn't. And even if I did, I wouldn't want you getting in the middle of things. No more running to my rescue, Miranda. Agreed?"

She frowned, but nodded. "Agreed."

"Then let's get out of here."

"I don't suppose we can walk out the front gate?"

"Sorry. We don't know who might be out there waiting for us to make an appearance." He hurried her toward the fence where his jacket still hung. "Ready for a leg up?"

"Ready."

"Try to drop fast this time. There will be people up and moving around by now."

"I'll do my best, boss."

Hawke smiled, brushing strands of Miranda's curly hair away from her cheeks. "I'm glad you finally understand how things work."

With that he hooked his hands around her foot and boosted her up to the top of the fence. As she disappeared over the other side, he did something he hadn't done in years. He prayed. Not for himself, but for Miranda. Surely a God like the one his parents had trusted in would be willing to listen to a selfless plea.

And maybe, just maybe, that same God would be willing to give second chances. If so, Hawke figured he needed one. The past few years had taught him how fleeting life was, speeding by so quickly that a man could be at the end of it before he ever realized he'd left the beginning.

After a decade spent chasing justice and revenge, Hawke had chosen not to kill the man who'd ordered his parent's death. He didn't regret letting Sang Lao live. Sometimes, though, he regretted the years he'd devoted to bringing the drug kingpin down. While his high school and college friends had wives and children and had settled into the routine of family life. Hawke had settled into nothing but the knowledge of his own mortality; had gained nothing but scars and the memories that haunted him in the darkest hours of the night.

Sometimes he thought it was too late to change that. Other times, he knew he had to try. As he scaled the wall, he prayed that maybe, just maybe, God would grant him what he knew he desperately needed—peace.

FOURTEEN

Miranda landed on the pavement with a thud, stumbled backward and fell in a heap on the ground. Again.

"You okay?" Hawke dropped down beside her, offering a hand and pulling her to her feet.

"Sure, and though I think I've got the fall down pat, next time, I'd prefer landing on my feet."

"Let's hope there isn't a next time." Hawke put his hand on her elbow, hurrying her along the sidewalk and back the way they'd come. Chiang Mai had come to life in the time that they'd been in Jack McKenzie's house. People filled the sidewalk, some rushing to their destination, some sauntering along. Cars, motorcycles and taxis sped by. As did the strange three-wheeled vehicles Miranda had noticed in Bangkok. Three wheels. Justin would have loved it. His entire life had revolved around threes. Three sips of every drink. Three bites of every food. Three of every shirt, every pair of pants he'd owned. The thought brought hot tears and Miranda blinked them away, sure that if she let them fall, they'd never stop.

"What do you call that?" She pointed to the vehicle, forcing her mind to something other than her nephew.

"A *tuk-tuk*."

"It looks like a giant motorized tricycle."

"It is." He sounded distracted, his gaze scanning the growing crowd. "When this is over, we'll ride in one. I'll take you to the floating market, show you some of the tourist sights and some that aren't so touristy."

"*If* this is ever over." She was beginning to doubt it would be.

"It will be. Jack didn't give me those names because one of them might be the leak we're looking for. He gave them to me because he knows one is."

"Maybe, but I don't trust him. He used you."

"Yeah. And he and I are going to have a long talk about it. *After* I find the leak. But my gut says he's telling the truth."

"What if it's wrong?"

"It hasn't failed me yet." He frowned, glancing over his shoulder. "You did a pretty good job keeping up on our run yesterday. You ever run in the morning?"

"For exercise? Do I look like I do?"

"You look just like a woman should." His eyes met hers and Miranda's pulsed leaped at the admiration she saw there. "But I'm thinking now is as good a time as any to start a morning routine."

He yanked her in front of him, released his hold and gave her a gentle shove. "Go."

She ran, her feet pounding the pavement, Hawke right on her heels issuing directions in a calm, tight voice that worried her more than loud shouts would have. Someone was following them. That much was clear. Who or why remained to be seen.

Miranda fought the urge to look back over her shoulder, sure that if she saw someone coming up behind them, she'd freeze and get Hawke and herself killed.

"Come on, babe. You can move faster than this." Hawke urged her on and Miranda took off in a full-out sprint.

"Left."

She followed Hawke's command, turning left into a narrow alley and almost running headlong into a fence.

"Whoa." She skidded to a stop, her breath heaving from her lungs, her eyes scanning the trash-clogged area she stood in. "We're trapped."

"You're looking at it from the wrong perspective. We're not the ones trapped. They are."

They?

A shout sounded from somewhere close, the sound skittering along Miranda's nerves.

"Come here." Hawke grabbed her hand, pulling her to several trash cans overflowing with garbage. "Get behind these and don't come out."

She hurried to do as he said, squatting down behind the garbage, nearly gagging as the smell hit her nose. Rotted food littered the ground near her feet and a dead rat stared at her through flat, black eyes, maggots crawling through its fur in white wiggling masses. She looked away, her stomach rebelling at the sight, the stench and her fear.

Another shout followed the first, this time accompanied by pounding feet and muttered words. It sounded like an army was entering the alley. Miranda's pulse raced, adrenaline pouring through her so that she wanted to leap from her hiding place and run for safety.

Please, get us out of this in one piece, Lord.

The prayer had barely formed when silence descended. Thick and filled with malice, it surrounded Miranda, taunting her, daring her to peek out from behind her hiding place. She bit her lip, her muscles rigid, her breath stalling in her throat. A soft sound drifted on the rank air, a shuffling footstep that made the hair on the back of Miranda's neck stand on end.

Her hands fisted, her fingernails digging into her palm. The sound came again, this time closer, and Miranda was sure someone was standing on the other side of the trash cans. She didn't dare move. Didn't dare breath. Just slowly lifted her gaze, prepared for whatever she might see. *Whoever* she might see. No one was there. Not even a hint of a shadow drifted across her vision.

Seconds stretched into minutes. Minutes into eternity. Perhaps they'd gone to search another area. Or maybe they were waiting for Miranda or Hawke to make the first move.

A hoarse cry broke the silence, the sound so loud and so close, Miranda jumped. There was a crash, another shout, a thud. Muffled grunts. Muttered words. Something slammed into the trash can, releasing an avalanche of papers and garbage.

And then it was over.

Nothing moved, the air in the alley so still and thick Miranda was sure she would suffocate.

"Come on out." Hawke's voice broke the silence, the relief of it sweeping through Miranda in waves. She scrambled to her feet, her gaze searching for Hawke.

He stood at the far end of the alley, a man's body at his feet. Another lay a few yards away. A third slumped against a pile of garbage, blood seeping from his mouth and dripping onto the grimy pavement.

"Are they dead?" Miranda whispered the question, not really sure she wanted to hear his response.

"No, but they will be if they don't give me some answers." His eyes were icy with rage, his jaw set, each word a staccato beat that jabbed into the air.

"You're not really going to kill them." It was a protest more than a question.

"No? Watch me." He reached down, dragged the man up by his shirtfront and said something in Thai.

The man shook his head, speaking in quick, frantic gasps.

Hawke smiled, the expression so filled with malice Miranda took a step back. He spoke again, releasing the man's shirt and grabbing his neck.

"Hawke! No!" Miranda raced forward, horror at what she was seeing overriding fear, common sense and the self-preservation that had kept her still and quiet behind the rotting garbage and rat carcass.

"Stay there, Miranda." Hawke didn't raise his voice, his focus never straying from the man whose life he held in his hand, but his words were a steel-edged blade that might cut quickly and ruthlessly if she didn't obey.

A little more pressure and the man's air supply would be cut off, his tan skin already growing dusky and bluish, would darken. A lot more pressure and his trachea would be crushed, all hope of survival disappearing with his air supply. But there was no way it would come to that. No way Hawke would push things that far.

Would he?

Miranda didn't want to believe it could happen, but the image danced through her mind, sickening and real, the moment like a nightmare, her words sticking in her throat, her feet glued to the ground, indecisiveness holding her in place. She'd seen Hawke's rage, but he'd always maintained control. That didn't mean he couldn't or wouldn't lose it.

Trust him.

The thought came out of nowhere, so foreign Miranda wanted to ignore it. Trusting men wasn't what she did. Not anymore. She didn't plan to change that anytime soon. Especially not when the man was someone she barely knew. Yet somehow trusting Hawke at this moment, in this instance, seemed right; believing that he wouldn't coldheartedly murder a man seemed more possible than believing he would.

She stayed put, watching with a sort of numb detachment as the man Hawke held twisted and struggled in his grip, his skin growing a shade darker, his eyes bulging in terror. Finally, just as Miranda was sure he'd pass out, he spoke, the words rasping out in a waterfall of unintelligible sound.

Hawke must have understood. He smiled again, his eyes that of a predator, cold, hard and completely focused as he dropped the man to the ground in a puddle of coughing, choking humanity. Hawke spoke in harsh, angry tones and the man nodded, scrambling away, rushing from the alley.

Only then did Hawke turn his attention back to Miranda. His eyes gleamed cold and unforgiving, but his voice was calm, almost cajoling. "Come on, babe. We've got to hurry."

He held out a hand and Miranda moved toward him, her legs shaking so hard she was afraid they'd give out. "What did he tell you?"

"Not as much as I'd hoped he would. A drug dealer named Mahang Sharee hired him to bring me in. Apparently, Sharee has my brother and wants to negotiate a trade."

"Attacking us in an alley is a funny way to open up negotiations."

"Yeah, it is that, isn't it? They would have killed me and brought my body in if they could have managed it. Offering my brother in trade was plan B."

"In trade for what?"

"Me. I turn myself over. My brother goes free."

"Not really."

"No," he spoke quietly, his hand on her shoulder in unconscious support. "And they know I know it. They also know I'll do whatever it takes to have at least a chance of gaining Simon's freedom."

"What now?"

"We find Sharee."

"Do you have any idea where he is?"

"Last time I heard, he was over the border in Myanmar."

"That's pretty vague."

"Yeah, but I'm not worried. His man will pass along my message. In a few hours, I'll be hearing from him."

"And hopefully he'll lead you to Simon."

"Right."

"But what does Sharee have to do with what happened in Maryland? We're half a world away from Liam and Green."

"Half a world away from Green, but not from the Wa and that's who pays the bills for both men."

"The Wa?"

They reached the motorcycle and Hawke got on,

gesturing for Miranda to climb on after him. "They're a militia group based in Myanmar and make their money selling opium. Sharee is a big part of that. The DEA has been trying to bring him down for years, but every time they get close he disappears, or their informants do."

"Just like with Harold Green."

"Just like with him." Hawke squeezed her hand.

"So, the same agent leaking information to one is also leaking it to the other."

"We're thinking alike, babe. And I'd say Green and Sharee aren't the only ones who are paying for inside information. Our guy has got to be making a lot of money. The question is, what is he doing with it?"

"Putting it in a Swiss bank account?"

"Maybe."

"Where else could it be?"

"Used for something that Jack hasn't found yet."

"Like?"

"I don't know, but I plan to find out. Let's go check out some houses. A man's loyalties can be found in his personal space."

With that they roared out of the alley and into traffic, the motorcycle speeding past vehicles, exhaust fumes stinging Miranda's lungs. She clutched Hawke's waist, buried her head in the back of his shirt, trying to quiet the wild throbbing of her pulse and praying that Hawke was right, that they'd find the information they needed. That soon she'd be on her way home, heading back to the silent town house and her little business, to the life that had seemed enough until Justin's death, but that now stretched out before her, devoid of purpose.

No, that wasn't quite right. Her life wasn't devoid of

purpose, it was devoid of the certainty she'd had. In the years that she'd been Justin's primary caregiver, she'd been so sure of her place here on earth. Now that he was gone, she didn't know what direction her life would take, wasn't even sure how she could know if the direction she chose was the one God wanted for her.

She was determined to figure it out, though. Determined to do it right this time, to not hesitate when God put a task before her, to trust that He would guide her and keep her from making the same foolish mistakes she'd made in the past.

Of course, all her determination wouldn't mean a thing if she didn't make it out of Thailand alive. She prayed that she would, that she'd have another chance to mend fences with her sister, to create a stronger relationship with her brother, to live life to its fullest. No fear. No timidity. No shying away from what she knew was right.

Hawke took a sharp corner, the motorcycle tilting, the world tilting with it, colors and sounds so bright and vivid, Miranda closed her eyes and pressed closer to Hawke's back, inhaling his masculine scent. Her fingers dug into his side, her heart beating in time with his, her prayer for herself becoming a prayer for him, that he, too, would find purpose in the wild, crazy world he lived in. That God would touch his heart, heal his hurts and bring him safely through whatever trouble was to come.

That He'd bring them both through it.

Together.

The word floated through her head, stuck fast in her heart, making her feel less alone than she had in a long, long time.

And that, Miranda thought, was not a good thing.

FIFTEEN

Breaking into houses was easier than Miranda could have imagined. Still, she wasn't sure if she should be impressed or appalled that Hawke was so good at it. They entered the first apartment through the front door, sauntering through a lobby, into an elevator and onto the correct floor as if they belonged there. Hawke knocked twice, waited a few minutes and then set to work on the lock. Within minutes, he had the door open.

"There's no security system that I can see. Let's go."

"What if there's one that you can't see?"

"Then we're in trouble." He tugged her into the apartment, and closed the door behind them. They were standing in a beige living room. The carpet, walls and furniture all varying shades of light brown. A few pictures decorated the wall, but even they lacked color, the watery pastel prints commanding little attention.

"I don't think this is our guy." She whispered the words, though the house felt empty.

"No? Why not?"

"He's got no imagination and no drive. Look how bland this room is."

"Maybe it's that way because his time and creative energy is being used somewhere else."

"How can we know?"

"We search."

"For…?"

"For something that looks important."

An hour later, they'd found nothing more exciting than an application for a dating service and Miranda was more convinced than ever that the man who lived in the apartment wasn't the leak.

"I think we're wasting time." She shot a glance at Hawke who was sifting through a canister of flour, his dark hands coated in white powder.

He brushed them off, replaced the canister lid. "You've got good instincts, babe. Let's get out of here."

The next apartment was occupied, the woman who answered the door a fortysomething American with bleached-blond hair and a bright smile. "Yes?"

"Mrs. Austin?"

"Yes?"

"I'm Agent Randolph and this is Agent Johnson. We work with your husband."

"Is something wrong?"

"Not at all. We conduct a drug awareness program at the orphanage just outside of Chiang Mai. Do you know it?"

"I do. My friends and I visit there once a month."

"That must be why your husband said you might have something to contribute." Hawke smiled, his voice warm and friendly. He looked nothing like the man who'd nearly choked someone in an alley just a short time ago.

"Contribute?"

"We're collecting used books and toys to take over there later today."

"He must have forgotten to mention it, but I'm sure I've got some things here you can have. Come on in. I'll only be a minute." She opened the door wide, gestured for them to enter. "Would you like something to drink? Tea? Water? Coffee?"

"We're fine, and you don't need to trouble yourself looking for donations. We can come again in two weeks when we're scheduled to go back to the orphanage." Hawke smiled again, shooting a warning in Miranda's direction, his lies so smooth and convincing it was hard to believe he hadn't practiced them.

"Oh, no. You're here and I've got fifteen minutes before I need to leave for my women's club meeting. Let me just run and have a look." She disappeared down the hall, and Hawke moved quickly, crossing the room, scanning a bookshelf that stood against the wall, picking up a framed photo. Then another.

"Do you—"

He shook his head sharply, stepping away from the shelf as Mrs. Austin returned, her arms filled with books. "My kids don't read these anymore. I'd love for you to take them."

"Thank you. Do you mind if I use your restroom before we leave?"

"Go right ahead. It's down the hall and to the left."

"Thanks. And maybe I'll take you up on the offer of a drink if it's not too much bother."

"Of course. What can I get for you?"

"Water will be fine. How about you, Ms. Johnson?" There was a message in Hawke's eyes, but Miranda couldn't read it. Did he want her to accept? Refuse?

"Sure, a glass of water would be great." She managed to get the words out, saw the approval in Hawke's gaze and knew she was on the right track.

If this were a movie, she'd create a distraction so Hawke could search the rest of the house. But what kind of distraction? A fainting spell? A fire?

Maybe simple conversation was the best bet.

"Let me help you." She stood, following Mrs. Austin into her bright, airy kitchen. The dust motes dancing in the sunlight that streamed through the tall windows, the yellow walls and the crayon-art decoration on the refrigerator all reminded Miranda of home. "You have a lovely home."

"Thank you. It's not really what I'd hoped for when we got here. I'd been thinking we'd get a single family home, but they didn't have any available. How about you?"

"I'm in an apartment here, too."

"Have you been here long?"

"No. I just arrived."

"I thought so. My husband mentioned that a new agent was arriving soon. How do you like it so far?"

"Thailand seems like a wonderful place to work." She hoped Mrs. Austin wouldn't press for more, because she knew nothing about the kind of day to day work that went into being a DEA agent.

"It's a great country. Though I've got to say, I'm looking forward to returning home." She handed Miranda a glass of ice water.

"When will that be?" Miranda took a sip of water, hoping she could keep the conversation focused on the other woman.

"Another year. Maybe two. We were going to return

to Michigan this year, but my husband thought staying here for another year would help us financially."

Miranda's pulse accelerated at the mention of finances. If Hawke had been in the room, he would have known what to say, but he wasn't and Miranda struggled to come up with something that would keep the conversation moving in the same direction. "That sounds like a smart move."

"I guess so. We've got two kids to put through college, so I can't argue that it's not, but I miss home. My parents, sister and brother, their kids. I'd be happy to be back there with them again." She shrugged, smiled. "But you didn't come here to hear my life story."

"It's okay. I understand."

"Do you have a large family?"

"Not really, but what I have I already miss." That, at least, was the truth.

"Are we ready, Johnson?" Hawke strode into the room, the books in his hands, and accepted the glass of water Mrs. Austin held out to him.

"Yes." More than ready.

"Thank you for your donation, Mrs. Austin."

They said their goodbyes, stepped out into the hall, and walked away as the door clicked shut behind them.

Miranda almost sagged with relief. "I hope the next place is empty. I'm not good at pretending to be someone I'm not."

"I don't think we're going to have to worry about it." Hawke stepped past the elevator and pushed open a door that led to the stairwell, pulling Miranda inside.

"What do you mean?"

"The picture on the bookshelf was interesting."

"The family photo?"

"Yeah. But it wasn't the family that caught my attention. It was the background. It looked like it was taken in Russia. I found a photo album in their bedroom. One of those scrapbooks women like to keep. Labeled real nice. There were pictures of a trip the Austins took to Chechnya before they were married."

"You were in their bedroom?"

"Did you really think I was visiting the little boy's room, babe?"

"No. You just work fast. Do you think the trip to Chechnya has relevance?"

"I think someone very close to the Austins must live there."

"That's not surprising. Lots of people in the States have relatives in other countries."

"True, but I've got a feeling about this."

"What kind of feeling?"

"The kind that tells me Austin might have a place to send tens of thousands of dollars a year. The kind that tells me we'd better wait for his wife to leave and take a closer look at the apartment."

"I hope you're wrong. She seems so nice and they've got two kids"

"Life would be a lot simpler if the bad guys were easy to spot. Most of the time, though, they're just average people on the surface. Only further examination can ever reveal the truth."

"I hope further examination proves Austin is innocent. If he isn't, the entire family will be devastated."

"Bad choices lead to bad consequences. Not only for the one who makes them. We've got to accept that and do what we've set out to do. If that means bringing a nice woman's husband to justice, so be it." Hawke cracked the stairwell door open. "Mrs. Austin said she had a meeting. Let's see if she leaves on time."

It didn't take long. Fifteen minutes later, Miranda followed Hawke back into the Austin's apartment.

"You search the living room. I'll take the bedroom." Hawke disappeared down the hall and Miranda went to work. She had no idea what they were looking for, but she searched anyway, rifling through books, leafing through opened mail that lay in a pile on an end table. There was nothing suspicious, nothing unusual.

"I don't see anything in here." As she spoke, a sound came from the corridor beyond the closed apartment door. Miranda's heart leaped and she hurried toward the bedroom and Hawke.

He was kneeling in front of a bureau, looking at a piece of paper, but rose to his feet as Miranda entered the room. "What's up?"

"There's someone out in the hall."

"Probably someone returning to his apartment." As he said it, he grabbed what looked like a packet of letters and some old photographs from the drawer. "But we'd better take the back way out just in case."

"Back way? What back way?" Miranda was almost afraid to hear Hawke's answer.

"Right here." He unlocked a window, opened it, shoved out a screen and gestured Miranda over. "Come on."

Miranda peered out the window, saw a wrought-iron fire escape. "Wonderful."

"It could be worse."

A loud crash sounded from down the hall, and Miranda jumped, her eyes meeting Hawke's.

"Go!" He growled the words and Miranda obeyed, clamoring through the open window and onto the fire escape, her hands slippery on the cold metal, her body humming with adrenaline.

She didn't hear Hawke following her and didn't waste time looking to see if he was. Whoever was coming in the apartment wasn't being subtle about it and Miranda had no intention of sticking around to find out why. She raced down the fire escape, ran around the corner of the building and kept going, not sure where she was headed, only knowing she had to get away.

SIXTEEN

"Slow down, babe. People are starting to notice us." Hawke grabbed Miranda's arm and forced her to walk, shortening his own stride to match hers.

"Are they behind us?" Miranda's voice shook, but she looked almost calm, the pulse beating rapidly in the hollow of her throat the only indication of the terror she was feeling.

"If they are, they're staying back." He glanced over his shoulder as he spoke, but saw only the crowd of tourists and business people rushing to their destinations.

"But they could be there."

"They could be."

"I was hoping you'd disagree."

"Sorry, babe. I call it like I see it."

"You found something in the apartment, didn't you? Something that's convinced you Austin is the leak."

"Yeah, I did." He smiled, but the hair on the back of his neck was standing on end, alarm bells screaming that their pursuers were close.

"Come on. This way." He yanked Miranda into an alley, running now, keeping a few steps behind her, knowing that his body was poor protection from a bullet.

"Here!" He yanked her into a small fabric shop, the Indian proprietor taking in his and Miranda's appearance.

"Can I help you?" His English was precise and clear, his unhappiness obvious.

Hawke ignored him, moving through the store quickly, then into a back room, the man following along and complaining the entire time. A back door led out into another alley, and Hawke hurried Miranda into it. "Just a little farther. We're close to where I left the motorcycle."

"How close?" Miranda panted the words, her breath heaving with exertion as they ran full-out, her shorter legs moving twice as fast to keep up the pace.

"Really close."

"Did we lose them?"

"No. We just bought a couple minutes. Here we are." He nudged Miranda down a side street teaming with tourists and lined with vendors selling brightly colored hats, silk fans and fruit. Hawke wound his way through the crowd, his hand on Miranda's shoulder, his muscles tight, his skin prickling with awareness. Danger wasn't far behind them. He knew it. He could only hope the crowd would keep it at bay long enough to get Miranda to safety.

The street where he'd left the motorcycle was quiet, only a few locals and tourists wandering from shop to shop. Hawke hurried Miranda to the motorcycle, everything inside him saying they needed to get out of Chiang Mai *now*.

"Where are we going?"

"Home."

"Mine or yours?"

"Mine."

"In Bangkok?"

"Mae Hong Son."

"Where is that?"

"You ask a lot of questions, babe."

"Maybe if you gave more answers I wouldn't have to." She climbed onto the motorcycle behind him, her hands wrapped around his waist, small and warm and more familiar than they should have been after only a few days. It seemed they'd known each other much longer than that; a bond had formed between them, one that spanned more than a few dozen hours, a few shared moments and a common goal.

Hawke shook his head, denying the thought. There could never be a bond between people as completely different as he and Miranda.

He turned the ignition, starting the motorcycle just as two men rounded the corner of the street, their gazes scanning the area and settling on Hawke and Miranda. A flash of metal warned Hawke seconds before the pavement exploded just feet away from the motorcycle.

Miranda screamed, her fingers digging into his sides as Hawke gunned the engine and headed toward the approaching gunmen.

"Are you crazy? You're going to get killed!" Miranda shouted the words, hoping to penetrate whatever crazed fog Hawke was in.

"Keep your head down and hold on." His shouted reply did nothing to ease the horror that squeezed the air from her lungs, and cut off another scream.

She could see the men clearly—their tan complexions, their dark, cold eyes, the grim determined expressions on their faces.

Their guns.

They took aim. Fired. A bullet whizzed by. Another slammed into the sidewalk. Someone screamed, the sound echoed by another and another. People dove for cover, hiding behind cars, diving onto the pavement, protecting themselves in whatever way they could.

But Hawke didn't seem concerned about protection. He just kept going, driving straight toward the shooters, determined to run them down, accelerating so that wind tore at Miranda's hair and stung her eyes, nearly blinding her. Tears streamed down her cheeks but she couldn't close her eyes, couldn't force herself to look away from the horrifying tableau.

The men dove for cover as Hawke raced toward them, their guns firing, the bullets going wild. Miranda was sure that at any moment Hawke would slump forward, blood streaming from a bullet wound, the motorcycle crashing onto the pavement and skidding to a stop. She expected to feel the impact of a bullet tearing through her own flesh, and wondered if it would throw her off the cycle. If she would even be alive to find out.

Then they were rounding a corner, putting a building between themselves and the gunmen, and the sound of screams, of gunfire, of panic disappeared under the chugging rumble of the motorcycle.

Shock kept her silent. That was the only explanation Miranda could think of for not saying what she was thinking—that Hawke Morran had almost gotten himself killed. Minutes passed as buildings and shops gave way to houses and thick grassland. Terraced rice fields gleamed in the sunlight, attended by women wearing sarongs and straw hats. Dark clouds darkened the horizon, giving the world a sinister atmosphere despite the bright sun shining in a brilliant blue sky.

Everything seemed sinister. The man using water buffalo to plow a field. The thatched huts that stood on spindly legs above thick green foliage. The women walking along the side of the road, baskets held close to their bellies or perched on their heads. All had the potential for hidden danger. Another attack could come from any direction at any time and Hawke might very well run right into it again.

Miranda's heart beat faster, her body shaking with fear she no longer seemed able to control. A few scattered buildings dotted the landscape, signs jutting up from paved parking lots filled with buses and cars. Hawke pulled into one, stopping the motorcycle next to a gas pump and filling the tank.

Miranda could feel his gaze as he worked. She knew he was studying her but she didn't meet his eyes.

"You're still shaking." He pulled her off the bike and wrapped his arms around her, pressing her head against his chest as he murmured something in Thai, his voice so warm, so filled with concern, she wanted to dive into it, eke out all the comfort it offered.

"I've never been so scared in my life."

"But it's over now and you're safe." His hands smoothed down her hair and rested on her waist, his fingers tracing patterns on her back.

"I'm safe, but you almost got yourself shot trying to run those men down. For what? Revenge? Would it have been worth it if you ended up dead on the street?"

"Is that what you think? That I was trying to run them down?" His arms dropped away and he took a step back, all the concern, all the warmth gone from his voice.

"Weren't you?"

"Is that the kind of man you think I am? One that would risk your life to carry out a vendetta?" His eyes were storm-cloud gray, his expression shuttered.

Did she? Over the past few days Hawke had never done anything to jeopardize Miranda's safety. At times when he might have abandoned her, he'd stuck close, slowing down to accommodate her even when that meant risking his own safety. "Not my life. Yours. And I just thought that in the heat of the moment—"

"In the *heat of the moment* you thought I would trade your safety for revenge? That's supposed to make me feel better?" He spit the words out, disgust curling his lip and hardening his jaw.

"But you rode right toward them. You could have just turned and driven away." Her words were a lame attempt to justify what she'd believed, but even as she spoke them she knew they had no weight, no meaning.

"And have you shot in the back while we rode away? I took them by surprise. They were expecting retreat. I attacked. It was enough to get us to safety." He climbed back on the motorcycle as he spoke, his shoulders stiff, his tone harsh.

"I—"

"Get back on the bike. We've got hours to go before we make Mae Hong Son."

"Hawke—"

"Get on the bike." He bit out each word, anger making his scar stand out stark white against his dark skin, his gaze so cold and implacable that Miranda knew the conversation was over.

She climbed on behind Hawke, putting her hands on his waist. He tensed beneath her touch, his muscles unyielding as he started the engine.

Miranda was sure he'd pull back out onto the road, but he drove toward one of the many vendors set up in the open stalls instead and called to a young woman selling wide-brimmed straw hats. She hurried over, carrying a hat and a scarf made of red Thai silk. They bantered back and forth for a moment before Hawke exchanged a few coins for the hat. As soon as the woman walked away, he turned in his seat and faced Miranda with an expression devoid of emotion. "You're getting a sunburn."

"I'll be okay."

He ignored her comment, turning his attention to the hat, pulling the silk over its crown and pushing it through slats in the straw on either side. When he was finished, he placed it on Miranda's head, tying the silk snugly beneath her chin.

"Thank you."

He nodded, turning away without comment.

His anger had been understandable. His kindness nearly broke Miranda's heart.

As they pulled out onto the road, she felt a loss she couldn't explain, her stomach sick with the knowledge that she'd hurt a man who'd been doing everything he could to protect her. She wanted to apologize, but the roar of the motorcycle and her own guilt kept her from speaking. What could she possibly say that could make things better? How could she possibly explain her thoughts?

She didn't know, so she remained silent as the miles passed and the distant clouds moved closer.

SEVENTEEN

They drove into the downpour, a heavy sheet of rain slapping Miranda's shoulders and pinging off the pavement. Where everything had been dry, there was now half an inch of water, the fields and road swimming in it. Miranda thought Hawke would press on, driving through the sudden onslaught.

Instead he pulled the motorcycle to the side of the road. "Those trees will provide some cover. Let's go."

He got off the motorcycle, motioned for Miranda to do the same, then started across the field, heading toward two distant trees whose thick fronds provided a canopy of sorts. Leaves and branches weren't going to do much good—Miranda was already soaking wet—but pointing it out would be a waste of time, so she followed Hawke, the world reduced to slashing rain and green grass, gray skies and splashing puddles. Ankle-deep water sloshed against her legs as she walked, seeping into her shoes, socks and jeans until she felt waterlogged, her legs heavy, her body moving in slow motion. The idea of stopping where she was and sitting in the wet grass while the rain poured down appealed a lot more than continuing toward the trees.

She kept going anyway, her feet sinking into mud and muck, her nose filling with the loamy scent of wet earth, creatures scurrying in front of her, bugs, rodents and birds taking flight as she moved toward them.

Finally, she made it to the trees, ducking under low-hanging leaves and into a relatively dry patch of earth and grass. Hawke had the motorcycle parked near the trunk, and was crouching in front of his pack, rummaging through it.

He looked up as Miranda entered the shelter, his silvery eyes unreadable. "As soon as the rain stops, we'll get back on the road."

"How long do you think that will be?"

He shrugged, turning his attention back to the pack. "Fifteen minutes. An hour. More. It's hard to say during the rainy season."

"I'll pray it's less time rather than more."

Hawke didn't comment, just pulled a packet of papers and photos from under his shirt, wiped the moisture from them and wrapped them in a plastic bag he'd pulled from his pack. When he was finished, he closed the pack and held it out to Miranda. "Use this as a pillow and rest for a while. We've got another five hours of driving ahead of us and I don't want to have to stop again unless we have to."

The words were curt and Miranda took them for what they were—a not-so-subtle hint to stop talking. She wanted to ignore them, wanted to keep trying to fill the hollow silence, but knew being quiet would be the smarter choice. Her words had done enough damage for one day.

She grabbed the pack, laid it on the grass and dropped down beside it, the ground surprisingly soft beneath her as she stretched out on her side. The patter of rain above, the splash of it beyond the leaves became a quiet lullaby, the humid air a blanket. Miranda's eyes drifted closed, but she forced them open, afraid to sleep; afraid of what she'd wake to.

"Let yourself go for a while, Miranda. I'll make sure you're safe."

She jumped at the sound of Hawke's voice, saw that he had moved closer and was sitting with his arms crossed in front of his chest, his damp hair falling across his cheeks.

Miranda couldn't see his expression, but sensed a softening in him. If she were going to apologize now was the time to do it. "I'm sorry I hurt you. I wasn't thinking clearly."

"It's hard to think with bullets flying by your head."

"You managed it."

"I'm used to it."

"So you do this kind of thing a lot?"

"Not if I can help it, but tracking down drug dealers often puts a person in situations he'd rather avoid."

"How long have you been working with the DEA?"

"Nine months. But I've been hunting down drug traders for ten years."

"That's a long time."

"A lifetime." He raked his hair back, tying it with a strip of leather he pulled from his pocket. His profile was strong, stark, devoid of softness, but his hand was gentle as he placed it over Miranda's mouth. "Now be quiet and sleep. We've got a long day ahead of us."

She tugged his hand away from her mouth, holding it as she studied his face, his scar, his long fingers and broad palms, everything about him completely familiar and absolutely foreign. "I really am sorry. I should have known you wouldn't put yourself in danger without good reason."

He shook his head, smiling a little. "Will you spend the rest of our time together worrying more about me than you do about yourself?"

"Trust me, I'm worried about myself."

"Yet it didn't even occur to you that turning the bike around and riding away from the shooters could easily have gotten you killed."

"Given enough time I probably would have thought about that."

"Maybe, but I doubt it." He skimmed the knuckles of his free hand down her cheek. "You've asked a lot of questions. Now, I have one for you."

"What is it?"

"The first night we met, you smelled like apples and cinnamon, so sweet and intoxicating I was sure I must be imagining it. Was it some exotic perfume designed just for you?"

"I'd been baking a pie. It's what I do. Bake things." She was stammering, her face heating.

"Bake things?"

"I own a bakery in Essex. Or I did. Now that Justin is gone…"

"What?"

"I opened it mostly for him. To give him a place other than the house where he could feel comfortable. We spent a lot of time there together. I'm not sure I want to keep working in a place that holds so many memories."

"Good memories?"

"Mostly. Some not so good."

"It was hard raising your nephew."

"No. Raising him wasn't hard. What was hard was knowing Justin was locked inside himself and that there was no key to open his mind and let him out."

"You were his key, I think."

"No. I wanted to be, but even I couldn't manage that. I use to pray all the time that he'd be cured, that some miracle drug would be found and Justin would become the child he use to be."

"But he is now. After death, a person is freed from disease, from heartache, from pain. Isn't that what you believe?" He watched her, his stillness and intensity making Miranda wonder what it was he was seeking.

"Yes. It's part of what I believe, anyway."

"What's the other part?"

"That dying means eternity spent with God."

"For some."

"For anyone who believes. It's about faith. Relationships. Love."

"Perhaps that's the part I've been missing."

"Belief?"

"No. I believe there is a God. How could I not? Relationship and love are what I haven't quite figured out."

"And faith?"

"I'm learning." He stretched, pulled his cell phone from his pocket. "Let's see if this works. It's past time I contacted Jack. And I should be hearing from Sharee soon, too. News of my brother will be welcome."

Miranda nodded, settling back onto the ground, her skin chilled from the wet clothes she wore.

Hawke's quiet words were barely audible, his face turned away. Miranda let her mind wander, her thoughts drifting on the pattering hum of rain. Thoughts that only seemed able to go in one direction—Hawke.

Miranda had known atheists. She'd known agnostics. She'd never known a man who believed in God but had no faith in Him. Who understood the existence of the creator but didn't have a relationship with Him.

But, then, she'd never known a man like Hawke.

Her own father had professed to be a Christian, his pilgrimages to Christmas and Easter services fulfilling whatever need he had to live that faith. Every man she'd ever dated had been the same, professing Christianity only when it suited him.

Hawke was different. Whatever he believed, he lived. Whatever road he took, he stayed on it until he reached the end. He wouldn't sit on fences, waffle between ideals or change his mind with his moods. He was constant, steady, someone who could always be counted on to know the truth and live it.

She closed her eyes, praying for Hawke as the rain continued to fall and her mind finally gave in to sleep.

"We've got to get moving." The words drifted into Miranda's dreams, pulling her from sleep.

She jerked upright, her heart racing, stars dancing in front of her eyes at the quickness of the motion.

"Slow down, babe." Hawke put a hand on her shoulder, holding her steady.

"I'm ready."

"Just sit for a second. Here." He took a banana and a bottle of water from his pack and handed to her. "Eat."

"What about you?"

"I already had something."

Miranda took a bite of banana, swallowed some water and stood. "Now I really am ready."

"Finish the banana, then we'll go."

"Are you always so bossy?"

"Are you always so combative?" He smiled as he said it, pulling the water from Miranda's hands and taking a drink from it before passing the bottle back to her.

"Only when I'm with you."

"Then I guess we bring out the best in each other."

Miranda laughed and took another bite of banana. "If this is my best, I'd hate to see what my worst is. How long did I sleep?"

"Two hours. Longer than I would have liked, but we both needed the rest."

"Were you able to reach Jack?"

"Yeah. He gave me some information about Austin. Most of it I'd already guessed. He was adopted from Russia when he was six. According to birth records his parents were from Chechnya."

"What about the photos?"

"I described them, but there's not much Jack can take from that. He's going to do some research. See if he can find any connection between Austin's paternal or maternal family and the militia groups in Chechnya."

"What are you thinking?"

"I'm thinking that if Austin is the one selling information, he's using his earnings to fund one of the groups fighting for power in the country where he was born."

Hawke grabbed the pack, stood and extended a hand to Miranda. "We've got to get moving. I want to reach Mae Hong Son before nightfall. We'll both be safer there."

"Don't worry, I'm as anxious to get there as you are."

"Good. Because if something happens to me, if we

get separated, I want you to find your way there. People in town know me. They'll be able to get you to my home. That's the only place where you'll be safe."

"What's going on? Why are you telling me this?"

"Because things are about to get a whole lot worse then they've been. Mae Hong Son is close to Myanmar. Myanmar is the Wa's playground. And the Wa and I go back a long way."

"Ten years."

"Yeah. I've been doing everything in my power to close them down since the day they murdered my family. And they've been doing everything in their power to keep me from succeeding. Come on, we've wasted enough time." He turned away, pushing the motorcycle out from under the trees.

Miranda raced after him, splashing through puddles, his words replaying over and over again as she climbed onto the back of the bike and they began their journey again.

EIGHTEEN

By the time they reached the outskirts of Mae Hong Son, it was dark and Hawke could feel Miranda sagging against his back, her forehead resting on his shoulder, her hands barely holding his sides. She'd been exhausted when they left Chiang Mai. Now her fatigue seemed a living thing, weighing her down and threatening to topple them both from the motorcycle.

"You still with me?" He shouted the words over the rumble of the motor. Miranda lifted her head, her grip tightening a fraction, his words apparently dragging her from the half-sleep state he'd suspected she was in.

"Where else would I be?"

"In a dream a whole lot nicer than our reality."

"It's kind of hard to dream when you're sitting on the back of a motorcycle." Fatigue and dehydration added a raspy edge to her voice and Hawke winced in sympathy. It had been two hours since their last stop for fuel. Longer since their last drink of water. The fact that she wasn't complaining didn't mean Miranda wasn't suffering. But as much as he sympathized, Hawke couldn't make himself stop.

The stakes weren't the same as they had been in

Bangkok and there was no time to waste on rest and re-freshment. Sharee had upped the ante when he'd taken Simon. If the drug lord hadn't called Hawke's Mae Hong Son compound already, Hawke would find a way to send word to him. It was time to set the meeting. The sooner the better.

"Is that Mae Hong Son?" Miranda interrupted his thoughts, her words pulling him from the dark path his mind was traveling.

"Yes."

"It's beautiful."

Hawke looked at the town where he'd spent the first ten years of his life—the mountains dark shadows against the night sky, the houses and buildings a cluster of lights, the night unfolding in a hushed expectancy. There was mystery here, carried in on the mountain mist that shrouded the town in the morning and evening, gathering force from the thick jungles that surrounded the tiny place. There was, he supposed, beauty in that, though it had been years since he'd taken the time to notice it. "Yes, it is. More so during the day, though, when you can see the mountains and jungles, the water and sky."

"Then it won't just be beautiful. It will be breathtaking." She paused for a moment, her body shifting slightly as if she were trying to get a better look. "It's smaller than I thought."

"Most people say the same. Mae Hong Son is a surprise. They expect a larger town, but are never dis-appointed in what they find here."

"What do they find?"

"It depends on what they seek. Some find peace, a sense of oneness with nature. Others find proof of God in His creation. Too many find easy access to heroin." His biological father had been one of those, his death from overdose taking him just a year after he'd married Hawke's mother. Hawke hadn't known him enough to mourn him. Patrick had been his father, his mentor, his friend. He, Hawke did mourn and probably always would.

"That's sad."

"More so for the families that are destroyed by it."

"You sound as if you know."

"My father became an addict here. It killed him."

"Is that why you're so determined to destroy the Wa?"

"No. He chose to give his life over to his addiction. My stepfather, mother and sister did not. They were killed in cold blood as an example of what would happen to businessmen who refused to work with the Wa." Even now, so many years later, saying it filled Hawke with fury. His hands tightened on the handle-bars; his jaw clenched to keep more words from pouring out.

"I'm so sorry, Hawke."

"I am, too, but the past is just that. The present is for the living."

"If it is, then why are you trying so hard to avenge the murder of your family?" If anyone other than Miranda had asked the question, Hawke would have ignored it. But there was something about Miranda that demanded answers. Even when Hawke wasn't quite sure what those answers were.

"I didn't want revenge. I wanted justice."

"Sometimes they're the same thing."

"Maybe they are, but what happened to my family

demanded retribution." Or so he'd thought. Now, after years of fighting drug traffickers, he wasn't so sure that retribution would accomplish anything.

"Retribution isn't for us to demand."

"But if you could demand it from the drunk driver who killed your nephew, would you?"

She was silent for a moment and Hawke wondered if his words had poured salt in the wound of her loss. He opened his mouth to apologize but she spoke before he could. "Maybe."

It was an honest answer and more than what he would have given with a loved one's death still so raw and new. "And maybe if I'd devoted myself to something else, you and I wouldn't be here tonight."

He turned down the side road that led to his compound, the lights from Mae Hong Son disappearing from view as he drove in the opposite direction of the town, the darkness suddenly complete but for headlights illuminating the road.

"I thought we were going to Mae Hong Son."

"We're there."

"The town, I mean. It's behind us."

"I live a few miles outside of it."

"How many is a few?" The weariness in her voice was obvious and Hawke wished he had a different answer.

"Twenty."

"So. A half hour more. I can do anything for a half hour." She rested her head against his back again. He could feel the smooth curve of her cheek and jaw. He imagined her moss-green eyes and freckled skin, imagined driving her through the mountains of Mae Hong Son when the sun was shining and Sharee's men weren't after them. It was a dangerous thought. One he couldn't afford. Miranda wasn't the kind of woman who'd take to riding on the back of a motorcycle. She was more the type to stand in a sunny kitchen baking pies and humming hymns. That simplicity, that wholesomeness wasn't something Hawke wanted to taint with the darkness he carried in his soul.

He forced his mind to the conversation and away from what he shouldn't even be contemplating. "You can do whatever you set your mind to for as long as you need to."

"I think you have more confidence in me then I have in myself."

"Whatever it takes, babe." He glanced in the mirror, peering into the darkness behind them, his skin suddenly tight, his nerves shooting warnings to his brain. He saw nothing but blackness, heard nothing but the rumble of the motorcycle and his own quickening heartbeat.

But something was there. He sensed it as surely as he'd sensed trouble in the seconds before he'd been knocked unconscious in Essex. If Sharee's men were going to attack this would be the place to do it. Too far from town and from Hawke's compound to have their attack interfered with, no side roads for Hawke to lose them on.

He accelerated, pushing the motorcycle to speeds that were just short of reckless. The ill-kept road, bumpy and slick from rain, was an accident waiting to happen, but only the thought of Miranda, helmetless on the back of the cycle, kept him from pushing it to top speed.

"What's wrong?" Miranda's shout barely carried above the rush of wind and roar of the motor.

"Just a feeling."

"What kind of feeling?"

"The feeling that trouble is right behind us."

She shifted and Hawke was sure she'd turned her head to try and see whatever might be there. "I think you're right."

"You see something?"

"I think so. No headlights, but something darker in the blackness." She paused. "Or maybe not. It's hard to tell."

If she thought she was seeing something, Hawke figured she was.

"Hold on tight." He pushed the motorcycle harder, the bounce of wheels on the cracked and crumbling asphalt making him worry even more for Miranda's safety.

"I think it's a car. And I think it's gaining on us." Hawke sensed her panic in the taut, clipped tone of her voice and the painful grip she had on his waist.

Far in the distance, the compound beckoned—a pinpoint of light that might have been a star, a campfire, or headlights, but that Hawke knew was home. He cut the lights on the motorcycle, the world becoming a pitch-black tomb, then coasted to a stop.

With the engine off, he could hear the rumble of another vehicle speeding toward them.

"What's going on? What are we doing?" Miranda whispered the question, as if fearing that the sound of her voice might carry to those coming after them.

"We can't outrun them on this bike, but we may be able to outsmart them on foot."

"On foot? Are you crazy? We're in the middle of nowhere."

"No. We're not." He got off the motorcycle, and tugged Miranda off beside him. "See that light?" He turned her head, so that she was looking in the direction of the compound.

"The one that looks like it's a hundred miles away?"

"That's home. Gates, guns and guards I trust with my life. All we have to do is get there." He pulled the motorcycle into knee-high grass, laying it down so that a passing car would easily miss it.

"I like the sound of that."

"Come on." He moved deeper into the grass. "It won't take them long to realize I've pulled off the road and we're on foot."

"Then we'd better run."

"Exactly." Hawke grabbed Miranda's hand, felt her fingers link with his, her muscles tense. And then they were off, racing through thick grass toward the distant light of home, the sound of pursuit growing louder behind them.

"Do you think they'll see us?" Miranda was already gasping for breath and Hawke tightened his grip on her hand, afraid if he loosened it, he'd lose her in the blackness.

"I don't know. If they have night vision, we're in trouble."

"Night vision? As in those alien-looking goggles I've seen on the military channel?"

"Yeah."

"What's the likelihood they do?"

"Not high." But higher than he would have liked. The Wa could afford to furnish the best military equipment for their men. Hawke could only hope there hadn't been enough time for the crew coming up behind them to be outfitted with state-of-the-art technology.

"Maybe you should call your guards. Have them get out here to help us."

"We won't get a signal. Too many mountains. Too many trees."

"Maybe—"

"You need to save your breath, babe. We've got a long run ahead of us."

"Okay, but listen—" she panted out the words "—if I start slowing you down, you should go on ahead. You can get the help we need and bring them back for me."

"No."

"It makes sense. I won't be able to keep this pace up for long. We both know it. I'll never forgive myself if you're hurt because of me."

"Then you'd better keep up the pace, because I'm not going to leave you behind." There were plenty of things the Wa could do with a woman like Miranda. None of them were good. None of them were even pleasant. Hawke had seen those that the Wa owned— the blank-eyed prostitutes who worked on the outskirts of the poppy fields, hardened women whose beauty had faded with their innocence. He'd also seen the disease-ridden wasted bodies—the corpses of those who had no access to medical care and no one who cared enough to help them find it. Imagining Miranda among them left him with the same sick, hollow feeling the thought of losing Simon gave him.

"Hawke, I really think—"

"I really think you should do as I say. Save your breath. If you need to talk, talk to God. Ask Him for a miracle." They were going to need it, and for the second time in just a few hours, Hawke did what he'd never felt a need to do before. He prayed, hoping for help he really didn't believe he'd receive.

But somehow, as he pushed through thick foliage, Miranda panting along beside him, he had the strange sense that his prayer was being heard, that what he'd never quite been willing to accept had accepted him long ago. That all he had to do was reach out and grasp what was being offered. And more than anything, that's exactly what he wanted to do.

NINETEEN

Miranda couldn't decide which terrified her more—running blind through wet trees and knee-high grass or hearing the oncoming vehicle's engine growing louder with every step. Miranda didn't just want to run from it, she wanted to fly—spread invisible wings and soar above the danger like she had in a million nightmares. But this wasn't a nightmare, it was reality. And as much as she wanted to fly, all she could do was command her feet to move faster. Faster, though, seemed an impossibility. Her legs churned in slow motion, only Hawke's firm hold on her hand keeping her moving forward.

Blackness pressed in around her, stealing her breath, the sting of branches as they hit her face and the clawing tangle of vines and thorns her only clue as to the kind of landscape they were running through. She didn't need to see to imagine what might lurk in the depths of the foliage. Snakes. Spiders. Rats. Tigers.

Men with guns, ready to kill.

How far was Hawke's house? Miranda could no longer see the tiny light he'd had pointed out earlier and she wondered how he could possibly know they were running toward it. She wanted to ask, but knew he'd been right when he told her to save her breath. Her lungs were already on fire, her legs burning with the effort to keep pace with Hawke. Speaking would only use precious energy.

The engine cut off, the sudden silence so complete, Miranda stumbled.

"They know we're on foot." She gasped the words, terror pouring through her in futile waves of adrenaline. Her body was too tired to respond, her resources dried out and used up long ago.

"They passed the place we left the motorcycle before they stopped. They're going to have to back-track to find it."

"Are you sure?"

"Does it matter? We've got to run either way." His hand tightened around hers, his grip almost painful.

"It matters to me. The more time we have before they start after us, the better I'll feel."

"Then I'm sure. Now, stop talking. Sound carries a long way here."

As if in response to his words, the sound of an engine broke the stillness again, the slow, throbbing chug of it telling of a vehicle moving with care rather than speed. Hawke's pace quickened to a sprint, his hand jerking Miranda forward, her feet slipping in moist soil as she tried to keep up. He jerked her arm, keeping her from going down on her knees, but not slowing the pace.

Miranda's heart galloped, every breath seeming shallow and useless, every step a trembling torture. Just a few more minutes, just another mile and they'd be safe. She silently chanted the words to the beat of her pounding feet, but didn't believe them. She'd seen how far away Hawke's home was. Getting there would take more than a few steps and a few miles.

Sweats trickled down her forehead and into her eyes, mixing with the tears that she hadn't known were falling. Good out of bad. The Bible promised it. She believed it. But with Justin's death things had gone horribly wrong and all she saw was more trouble, more tragedy following. Where was the good that she so desperately needed to believe in? If she and Hawke were caught, there was no doubt they'd be killed, their bodies left for the beetles and vultures to devour.

Could there be any good in that?

Miranda didn't think so, but then, she couldn't picture the full tapestry of her life as God did, couldn't see the totality of His plan. If she could, maybe she'd understand all that had happened, all that was still happening, a little better.

Please, Lord. Get us out of this. I know You can. I want to believe You will.

She imagined the prayer drifting toward the sky, catching on the thick canopy of leaves above her and remaining there. But God wasn't in the sky, the heavens, someplace far above where she and Hawke raced through the jungle. He was here. In her mind, her soul, her heart. And in the quieting of her panic, she felt His silent reassurance. Whatever happened, God was in control of it. She'd just have to trust that His plan didn't include her body lying forgotten on the floor of the Mae Hong Son jungle.

The engine sounds stopped again, the silence an ominous warning. Miranda didn't dare speak, didn't dare ask Hawke how much distance they'd put between themselves and their pursuers, afraid her words would carry back to the men who followed.

Small drips of water landed on her shoulders and rolled down the neck of her borrowed T-shirt, each drop coming faster than the next. Rain. Despite the thick canopy of leaves, it poured down, making the ground even more slick than it had been.

Hawke slowed to a jog, pulling Miranda close to his side, his breath whispering near her ear. "They've found the motorcycle. The rain will slow us down, but it will slow them down, too, and make it harder for them to follow our tracks. We'll move slower, so we can keep as quiet as possible."

Thank you, God. Thank you, God. Miranda didn't speak the thanks out loud. Nor did she respond to Hawke's comment. The dark world was silent but for her harsh breathing and the roaring slash of rain falling through the trees. Whoever was coming after them was doing it silently, and Miranda willed her breathing to slow, her lungs to fill, afraid the gasping noise she made would draw their enemy toward them.

It seemed a lifetime passed while the downpour continued, the trudging half jog Hawke led them in more painful with every moment. Miranda's clothes were soaked, her hat catching on branches and trees. She wanted to tear it off and leave it lying in a soggy heap of straw and silk on the ground, but was afraid to leave behind evidence that she and Hawke had been there.

"We're close." Hawke leaned in again, wrapping his arm around Miranda's shoulders. "When we step out of the trees, we'll be on top of a hill. We've got make it to the bottom, then up another hill. All of it clear. There's no cover. No place for us to hide."

"Let's go." Miranda started forward, afraid if she thought too much about what he'd said, she'd be frozen with terror and unable to do what had to be done.

"Wait." He pulled her back against his chest, then let out a low, haunting whistle that reminded Miranda of a mourning dove's call.

Seconds later, a higher-pitched whistle sounded above the pouring rain. Distant, but clear, it could only be a signal of some sort.

"That's it. Apirak knows we're coming. Let's go." His arm dropped from her shoulder, his hand claimed hers and they were running again, racing through trees and out into an open field, rain still pouring, the sound of breaking branches and a muffled shout coming from somewhere behind them.

"Faster!" Hawke's shouted command spurred Miranda on, her feet slapping against waterlogged grass, a scream lodged in her throat. She wanted to let it loose, shout loud enough to wake whatever creatures had made beds for themselves in the thick grass and decaying leaves, but bit her lip to keep from doing what she knew she'd regret, the salty taste of her own blood a horrifying reminder of what would happen if Sharee's men found them.

The world tilted beneath her, the steep slope and slick ground forcing her to move faster than was safe. She tripped, her foot catching on something hard. Hawke's grip tightened, but even he couldn't stop her fall this time. She tumbled head over heels, the crash and crack of grass and branches a cacophony of noise that must have been audible for miles. Her body sliding in muck and puddles until she landed with a thud and splash in what felt like a small stream of rushing water.

Stunned, she lay still, starring up at the night sky, the sound of distant shouts and crashing footfall barely registering.

"Babe! You okay?" Hawke knelt beside her, black against the indigo sky.

"Yeah. Fine." But neither of them would be for long if she didn't get up and get moving.

"Are you sure?"

"Does it really matter? I can hear Sharee's men. They're getting closer. Let's get out of here." She started to rise and Hawke grabbed her hand, tugging her upright and dragging her into a run.

"See the blackness at the top of this rise? That's the fence that surrounds my compound. There will be men at the top, watching our progress. Men out here, too, probably coming up behind Sharee's men." He was barely breathing hard, and Miranda couldn't even force one word past her straining lungs.

She glanced up, nearly groaning when she saw the steep slope in front of them, her legs churning, her feet moving, but her body protesting every movement. "I don't see any lights."

"They've been turned out to keep us from being backlit while we're coming up the rise. We're already moving targets. We don't want to be well-lit moving targets. Come on, you've got more speed in you." He raced on and she had no choice but to join his frantic run up the steep hill, her legs burning, her lungs straining, stars dancing in front of her eyes.

Someone shouted, the Thai words unintelligible to Miranda, but Hawke must have understood. He pushed her down to the ground, throwing his body over hers as a barrage of bullets slammed into the earth a few feet away.

More gunfire followed, this time coming from somewhere in front of Miranda and Hawke's position. "My
men are covering us. Let's move."

Hawke stood in a smooth movement, bringing
Miranda with him as bullets continued to fly, the sound
deafening. There was no time to discuss a plan, no time
to think things through, just a swerving chaotic run
upward toward darkness and a house Hawke insisted
was there.

Then, as quickly as it had begun, the gunfire ended,
the silence ringing in Miranda's ears. Dark shadows
swarmed toward her from all sides, tall and deeper
black against the night. At first Miranda thought they
were a figment of her imagination brought on by her
oxygen-starved brain. Then the shadows took on more
solid form, men carrying guns, their faces shrouded by
the night, and Miranda realized how real they were.

"Hawke…" His name came out a high-pitched
squeak carried on her panting breath.

"Don't worry. They're my people." He didn't stop
running, though Miranda sensed a change in him, his
tight grip on her hand easing a little. Together, they
crested the rise of the hill and Miranda blinked. A clear
expanse of grass stretched toward a tall fence. Beyond
that, a house soared up toward the sky, its steep roof and
rounded turrets reminding her of the Gothic mansions
she'd seen on the covers of her mother's old romance
novels.

"This way." Hawke urged her along the line of the
fence then around a corner. A large gate slid open as they
approached and Hawke hurried Miranda into the
compound, the shadowy figures who'd surrounded them
following along. A soft slide of sound and a clang of

metal announced that the gate had closed, but Hawke didn't pause in his run, just continued up a long drive and onto a wide porch. There was still no light, but the front door of the house swung open before they reached it.

Hawke pushed Miranda in through the doorway, his gentle shove nearly toppling her. He moved in behind her, the quiet thud of the closing door followed quickly by blinding light.

As Miranda's eyes adjusted, she realized the hallway she stood in was filled with people. Six or seven men and women dressed in black and carrying the kind of weapons Miranda had only ever seen in movies, stared at her through dark almond eyes.

She tried to smile, but she was shaking too hard, her overworked muscles threatening to give out. Hawke said something in Thai and the men and women dispersed, some of them leaving the house, a few walking up stairs that led to the second floor. Finally, only one man was left, a small-built Thai man with a well-worn face and a short, compact body.

"Miranda, this is my business partner, Apirak. Apirak, Miranda Sheldon." Hawke made the introductions, his stormy eyes scanning Miranda's face, her soaked and mud-spattered clothes.

"Nice to meet you." Miranda held out her hand to Apirak and was surprised when he ignored the gesture and bowed instead.

She followed his example, dropping her head, and bowing from the waist. It was a mistake. As she straightened, the world spun, twisting and turning around her in a sickening array of colors. She swayed, knocking into a picture on the wall.

"Hey, careful there." Hawke's warm, callused palm gripped hers, his other hand resting on her shoulder and holding her steady.

"Sorry."

"For what? You just ran ten miles. I'd say you've got nothing to be sorry for."

"You go sit down. I'll bring some tea." Apirak's voice had a soothing melodic quality, his offer of tea making Miranda feel as if she'd stepped from a nightmare into normality.

"Orange juice would be better, Apirak, and some crackers. Also, see if we can find some dry clothes Miranda can use."

"Will do. It's good to have you back, Hawke." The Thai man gave Hawke a quick salute and disappeared down the hall.

"We'll go in the living room and wait there." Hawke started toward an open door, and Miranda tried to follow, but her legs refused to move.

"That sounds great, but I don't think I can move." The words came out half laugh, half sob, all the terror and anxiety of the past few hours welling up and spilling out in barely contained hysteria.

Hawke's expression softened, his eyes going from icy silver to warm gray. "Then I guess it's good you don't have to."

Before Miranda realized what he was going to do, he scooped her into his arms and strode through the open doorway.

TWENTY

"**P**ut me down. You'll break your back." Miranda wiggled against his hold, but Hawke ignored her struggles. She'd been serious when she'd said she couldn't move. He'd seen it in her eyes, could feel it now in her trembling muscles. They'd run close to ten miles at a breakneck speed. If she weren't exhausted he'd be surprised.

"You don't weigh enough to strain my back, let alone break it." He set her down on the sofa, water dripping from her hair and clothes onto the soft brown leather. "We need towels."

"Why? I'm kind of getting used to being soaking wet." Her teeth were chattering, her skin was ashen, but she smiled, the curve of her lips tugging at Hawke's heart in a way not much had in recent years.

"Yeah, well, I'm not going to let you catch pneumonia on my watch. Stay here. I'll grab some towels and be back in a minute."

"I'll come with you." Her eyes were dark with fatigue and worry as she started to rise.

He pushed her back down onto the couch, feeling the narrow width of her shoulder, the spastic tremors of overworked muscles. "You'll stay here and rest. Apirak is bringing juice. I want you to drink it all."

She blinked and Hawke was sure there were tears in her eyes. He wanted to sit beside her, throw an arm around her shoulder, let her know that they really were okay, but there were things that needed to be done. Sitting would accomplish none of them.

He strode from the room, calling for his housekeeper and not at all surprised when Doom stepped from the office across the hall, her lined face filled with concern.

"The *farang* is okay?" She spoke in Thai and Hawke responded in the same.

"She needs a hot shower, something to eat and some sleep. Can you make up the room at the top of the stairs?"

"I will. Have you heard anything of Simon?" The fear in her voice was obvious. Doom had been hired to help Hawke's mother the year Simon was born. She'd been working for the Morrans ever since.

"Sharee has him."

"No." She shook her head, tears filling her eyes and spilling down her cheeks.

Hawke took her hand. "Simon is tough. He'll be fine until I get to him."

"Let us pray you are right." She hurried up the stairs and Hawke followed, grabbing towels from the linen closet, then returning to the living room, a timer ticking in his head, counting down seconds and minutes. He had to get in touch with Sharee, arrange a meeting, get Simon back.

Miranda was where he'd left her, shivering on the couch, a glass in her hand, juice sloshing over the edges. Apirak leaned against the wall, his dark eyes meeting Hawke's.

"A call just came in on the office line. When you get Ms. Sheldon settled, we need to talk."

Hawke nodded, took the glass from Miranda's hand and placed it on the table before wrapping a towel around her shoulders. "My housekeeper will be down in a minute. She'll show you to your room."

"Where will you be?" Her eyes were mossy green and deeply shadowed, her dirt-stained face surrounded by heavy strands of dark hair.

"In my office. Apirak and I need to plan Simon's rescue."

"Good. Let's do it." She stood, swayed, managed to stay upright.

"Babe, you need to sleep."

"So do you." Her chin jutted, her eyes flashed, the stubbornness that had brought her through the rain and jungle not diminished by exhaustion.

"I will, but not yet."

"I don't want to—"

"You ready, miss? Your room is prepared and I have found some dry clothes you can change into." Doom peered in the open doorway, her face still streaked with tears.

Hawke knew there was no way Miranda would refuse her.

He was right. She hesitated, then nodded. "Sure. Thank you. You're going to be here when I'm done, right?" The question was directed at Hawke. He nodded, ushering her to the door as he spoke.

"I'll be here."

"And you'll let me know what the plans are? You won't go anywhere without me?"

"I'll let you know." But he would be going without

her. The next part of the mission was too dangerous, Miranda too fragile to risk taking her with him.

"You'd better. I'm just as much a part of this as you. And I have almost as much at stake."

"Almost? We could both lose our lives." Hawke followed her into the hall, surprised at the reluctance he felt at letting her out of his sight. He'd been hyper-vigilant about background checks since he'd been betrayed to the Wa last year and a young girl had been kidnapped from the compound. The men and women who worked for him were loyal to him and to the cause they fought for. Because of them, dozens of DEA and police raids had been carried out in the past year alone. Hawke had no reason to question Miranda's safety here. And still he felt reluctant to let her go.

"Yes, but my brother is safe in Essex. At least, I hope he is."

"If Green tries to harm your family, the police will get suspicious. He can't take the chance of a deeper investigation."

"I guess not." But she still looked worried, lines of fatigue and anxiety creasing her smooth brow.

Doom stepped in, sliding an arm around Miranda's waist and urging her to the stairs. "Come. You'll feel better when you're dry and rested."

Hawke resisted the urge to follow. Instead he stayed where he was, watching their retreating figures until the door to the room near the top of the stairs closed on them.

When he turned back toward the living room, Apirak was standing in the doorway. "You care for that woman."

It wasn't a question, but Hawke gave an answer anyway. "She saved my life."

"And so you dragged her halfway around the world with you."

"It was that or leave her to die at Green's hands."

"I don't know that being here is any safer."

True. But at least here she wasn't alone. Hawke didn't say as much. "What was the phone call about?"

"McKenzie called. He said you were right. Austin's maternal grandfather was killed by Russian troops eight years ago. There are rumors that he was the leader of one of the resistance armies. There is no concrete evidence, but McKenzie thinks it's interesting that that same army has grown fifty fold in the years since Austin was transferred here. They've got the best weapons. The best training. Before they were a ragtag group with more rhetoric than fight. Now they're a force to be reckoned with."

"Does he think he can get proof that Austin is funding the group?"

"He's working on it now. He's also keeping the search for you under his own control. The police here in Mae Hong Son will lay low until he tells them different."

"He's taking a risk with his career. If I go down, he'll go down with me."

"Maybe, but if he can pull this off and find the leak in his office, he'll be a hero."

Hawke nodded. "What else?"

"Austin is acting as if nothing is wrong. He reported your interview with his wife and is insisting on a full-out manhunt."

"Did he mention that anything was missing from his apartment?"

"No. Is there?"

"Yeah. I found letters and photos. The letters are written in a language I'm not familiar with, but I think they might be of interest to McKenzie."

"It seems odd for Austin not to mention them. There must be a reason for it."

"I'd say he doesn't realize McKenzie and I are working together and he thinks Sharee will take me out before I can figure out what the letters say."

"He's underestimated you, then." Apirak motioned toward the office. "We've sent Sharee's men running. We'd better get ready for his next move."

"It'll be a trade. Simon in exchange for me and the documents I took." Hawke moved into the large room behind his friend, the teak furniture, rich leather and wood floors both familiar and strange after so many months away.

"And Miss Sheldon. They'll want her, too."

"Too bad. I don't plan on bringing her with me."

"If we want to convince Sharee that he's got us on the run, you're going to have to act like you're willing to cooperate."

"When have I ever cooperated with drug dealers?" Hawke shrugged out of his T-shirt, grabbed another from the closet and pulled it on.

"You've never had good reason to. Now, they've got your brother. They'll think you will be willing to do just about anything to get him back."

"And I am. But that doesn't include risking an innocent woman's life."

The phone on the desk rang, cutting off further argument. Hawke picked it up, knowing before he heard the voice who'd be on the other end of the line. "Morran."

"You've got something I want." Sharee spoke in the guttural dialect of his hill tribespeople, his words hissing out like a serpent's warning.

"And you have someone I want. Where is my brother?"

"Alive. For now."

"Let me speak to him."

There was a moment of silence, then Simon's voice filled the line. "Took you long enough, bro."

Some of Hawke's tension drained away and he smiled. "If you hadn't gotten yourself into trouble, I wouldn't have had to come at all."

"For once, it wasn't me who started the trouble."

"I know. Things got out of control in the States."

"So much for starting a new life, eh?" There was a strain in Simon's voice that Hawke didn't like. It hinted at injury.

"Are you okay?"

"I'll be better once I get out of here."

"It won't be l—"

"Now you see that your brother is okay," Sharee interrupted. "Are you ready to listen?"

"Go ahead."

"You bring the pictures and letters you took from Austin and meet me at the village a half mile north of Wat Mueng Sai. You know it?"

"Yes."

"Bring the woman with you."

"No deal."

"Bring the woman or your brother will die." Sharee disconnected before Hawke could respond.

"How did your brother sound?" Apirak sat near the door, his shoulders tense. Like Doom, he'd been working for the Morrans for years and had become part of the family.

"Ornery as ever."

"That's good, then."

"Yes. Now I just have to make sure he stays that way."

"What's the plan?"

"We can't go in force. That's what Sharee will be expecting." Hawke crossed the room, pulled a rolled-up map from a shelf and spread it out on his desk.

"What do you suggest?"

"I'm thinking Sharee doesn't dare kill me until he makes sure I have the documents he's after."

"Agreed."

"So, we send out some of our guys and one of our ladies. While they're making slow progress toward the Myanmar border, you and I will move quickly. We get in the village, dispatch Sharee and his men, and find out if Simon is there."

"And if he isn't?"

"We get someone to tell us where he is. One way or another, we're taking control of the situation."

"I like the sound of that." Apirak's eyes gleamed in anticipation.

"Let's map out the quickest route. I want to be out of here fast."

"I'll map it. You go brief the team. Then you need to do what you told Miss Sheldon and rest." Apirak took a seat at the desk and grabbed a highlighter. "The sooner we get going. The happier I'll be."

"You and me both."

It took only minutes to get his men together, go over the plan and send them off to gather weapons and supplies. It took him even less time to ready himself. He'd done this many times before, though never with so much at risk. Infiltrating drug labs, gathering names, dates and other data to pass on to the police or DEA had been part of Hawke's life for a decade. At any other time, the idea of catching one of Thailand's most elusive drug cartels would have filled him with purpose. Now, his sole focus was on finding Simon and getting him home alive.

"Hawke?" Miranda hovered outside the open door to his office. Dressed in a snug black T-shirt and black cargo pants, her face freshly scrubbed, her hair pulled back from her pale, bruised face, she looked exhausted and much more lovely than she should have after all she'd been through.

"I thought you were sleeping."

"And I thought you weren't going anywhere." She gestured toward the backpack on his shoulders and the gun belt he'd strapped to his hips.

"I said I'd be in my office. I was. Now, I'm going to find my brother."

"And I'm supposed to stay here?"

"It's the only way to keep you safe."

"I've been safe with you."

Her trust in him pulled at Hawke, the intangible bond that seemed to draw him to her growing stronger. He stepped away, not trusting himself to keep from pulling her into his arms, inhaling the sweet scent that clung to her. "I've got to move fast, babe. You're not up to it."

If she'd argued, Hawke might have found a reason to separate himself and his emotions from Miranda, but she only nodded, leaning her shoulder against the doorjamb, her gaze filled with sadness and worry. "I know. I've just got this feeling that if we get separated, we'll never find each other again." She flushed, her cheeks a deep pink. "What I mean is—"

"No need to explain, babe. We started this as a team, and we'll end it as one. This part, though, I've got to do myself." He moved past her, stepping into the hallway, the need to be on the road warring with the desire to keep Miranda close.

"How long will you be gone?"

"Anywhere from a few hours to a few days."

"Days?"

"If it takes that long to find Simon."

"And I'm just supposed to sit around here and wait?"

"That's exactly what you're supposed to do."

"I'm not sure I like this plan."

"I'm not sure you've got any say in it."

Miranda opened her mouth, closed it and then shook her head, laughing, the sound peeling through the hallway and wrapping around Hawke's heart. He smiled, wishing he had more time to stand in the hall watching laughter play across her face. "What's so funny?"

"You and me. We've had this conversation too many times to count."

"That we have."

"I don't think we've agreed on anything since we met."

"We've only known each other a few days. There's still time."

"A few days. It seems like a lifetime." She'd stopped laughing, but her eyes still sparkled and Hawke wondered what it would be like to know her under different circumstances, at a time when danger didn't lurk at every corner.

"Has knowing me been that bad?" He meant to tease, but his words came out much more serious than he intended.

"Not bad. Just…familiar. Like you're an old friend I've suddenly reconnected with." She smiled, shrugged. "That's silly, I know."

"Is it? I've been thinking something similar." He cupped her neck in his hands, feeling the quiet thrum of her pulse beneath his fingers. "Listen, babe, no matter how long I'm gone, I want you to stay here. I don't want anything to happen to you while I'm out searching for my brother."

"I'll stay here as long as I know *you're* safe."

"I will be. This assignment is no different than any other I've been on. I've always managed to come through in one piece."

"Yeah? Well, that scar you're sporting says you've come pretty close to *not* coming out in one piece."

"God had other plans for me the day this happened." Hawke fingered the ridge of skin, remembering the day he'd almost been killed by men loyal to the Wa. Noah Stone had saved his life. Or at least that's what Hawke had chosen to believe. Now he felt different. It was too hard to believe that coincidence had brought first Noah and then Miranda into his life at just exactly the right time to save him. "He had other plans for me the day I met you, too."

He leaned forward, placed a gentle kiss on her lips, reveling in the soft warmth of her skin, the flowery scent of the shampoo she'd used. But this was dangerous territory—the kiss he'd meant to be nothing more than a thank-you, threatened to become something more. Hawke forced himself to step away. "I've got to go."

Miranda nodded, her cheeks flushed. "I'll stay here. And I'll be praying for you."

In years past, Hawke would have scoffed at the words. But things had changed. He'd changed. "I'll be praying for you, too, babe."

And he would. God had laid a foundation on Hawke's heart years ago when his mother and stepfather had taught him the truth of the Creator's love and sacrifice for humanity. Hawke had chosen to ignore their teachings, his anger and need for revenge overriding the quiet voice inside that yearned for peace.

He wouldn't ignore it any longer. God had saved him twice. Hawke could no longer turn his back on that. As he walked away, he gave his future to the one he finally believed held it in His hands.

TWENTY-ONE

The sun rose over Mae Hong Son in silent streaks of gold and glittering mist. Miranda watched from her bedroom window on the second-story floor, following the first faint glimmers of light as they spread across the domed mountains and the shadowy valley below. Hawke and Apirak had left hours ago and were now somewhere deep in the tangled jungles beyond the compound. Painted in greens and grays, the world seemed a place of both beauty and danger. A place where a man or woman could easily be lost. A place where bodies could lie unnoticed while scavengers tore the flesh from their bones and stole their identities.

Miranda shivered, the image not one she wanted to dwell on. As mysterious and dangerous as the misty jungle seemed to her, she knew Hawke and his men were at home there, that they'd moved through it, explored it for most of their lives. They'd be okay. She prayed they would be, anyway.

And she prayed they'd return quickly. Imagination was a poor companion. One that had haunted the restless sleep she'd fallen into. Nightmare figures had skulked just out of sight, their long shadows dancing across thick beds of leaves. Faceless bodies lying in dreadful stillness had created a path that stretched as far as her dream-self could see. She'd woken an hour after she'd fallen asleep and had been awake ever since, the silent house seeming to wait with her as dawn slowly arrived.

It was probably for the best that Hawke hadn't been able to tell her when he'd return. If she had expectations about how long his mission would take, she'd be watching the clock, worrying about every extra second it took for him to return.

Who was she trying to kid?

She *was* watching the clock. She *was* worrying. More and more as the seconds stretched into minutes, the minutes into hours. "Please, Lord, get them all back safely. Help Hawke find his brother quickly. Keep all of them from injury and harm."

She whispered the prayer, her voice sounding strangely out of place in the quiet house. The moment, her plea, reminding her of the time she'd spent at the hospital standing vigil over Justin's failing body. Then she'd been alone, too, Lauren gone home to sleep, convinced that Justin was too far gone to need her. Miranda hadn't been able to leave him, though, and she'd sat through the dark, quiet night, listening to muted hospital sounds and the constant beep of machinery until night had turned to day and day to night again.

How long she'd stand here, staring out into the morning, remained to be seen. Obviously, doing so wouldn't do Hawke or his men any good. It would only lead to more worry and tension, but Miranda couldn't seem to leave her vigil, her mind jumping from thought to thought, her heart beating a ragged, unhappy rhythm.

"Miss?" A soft knock sounded on the door and Miranda turned to see Hawke's housekeeper stepping across the threshold. "Will you have some breakfast?" Her English was flawless, her accent just slightly thicker than Hawke's.

"No, thank you."

"You must eat something. I'll make you coffee and toast. Maybe some fruit. You like pineapple?"

"Yes, but…" Miranda let the protest die. She didn't have the energy or the will to argue. "That's fine. Thank you."

"Shall I bring it up for you?" The woman's dark eyes were filled with the same worry Miranda was feeling. That, rather than any desire to leave the room, made her step toward the door.

"I'll come down."

"We will have coffee together while we wait." She smiled, her lined face creasing. "I am Doom."

"I'm Miranda." They stepped out into the hallway together and moved down the steps.

"You met Hawke in the United States."

"Yes." Though she wouldn't exactly call what had happened a meeting. They'd been thrown together had stayed together, and now not having him nearby left her anxious and antsy.

"He's a good man, but it is time he stopped fighting his battle and settled down. It is what his mother would have wanted for him. I think it is what he wants for himself."

"Is that why he was in the United States?"

"Yes, he had hopes of expanding the export company he and his brother own. Eventually bring Simon to the States. Thailand is dangerous for the Morrans, now. So many people do not appreciate the work they do."

"Exporting goods?"

Doom cast her a curious look. "That's the business Mr. Morran started. The boys have done quite well with it, but it's not what has gained them enemies." She gestured Miranda into a bright kitchen and pulled out a chair at the round teak table there. "Sit here."

"Then what *has* gained them enemies? His work against drug dealers?"

"Yes. Hawke has invested time and money in that pursuit. This compound, the people that work for him here are all part of that. Hawke has built a business much different than the one his stepfather began. Its sole purpose is to fight against the Wa. You know the Wa?"

"Hawke mentioned them."

"A bad group." Doom shook her head as she placed a plate of toast and fruit in front of Miranda. "They control many exporters to one extent or another, paying money to have their heroin shipped out of the country. Mr. Morran, he wanted nothing to do with that. When the Wa approached, he went to the police and turned in the local man who was working for them. A few nights later he, his wife and daughter were dead."

Miranda's stomach clenched and she pushed the toast away. "That's terrible."

"It was a very terrible time. Simon was only thirteen, staying with a friend for the night. That was what saved him."

"And Hawke?"

"Away at school in the States, getting his master's degree. He flew back from college as soon as he heard and has been here ever since, going after every drug dealer, every courier." Doom shook her head again. "That's what his life has been about. I think he is ready for something different."

"Then we need to pray he gets an opportunity to have it."

"Pray. Yes. That's something I've been doing every day since I came to work for the Morrans."

A sound from the front of the house interrupted the conversation. An opening door, footfall, loud voices. Miranda jumped up from the chair, racing into the hallway after Doom.

What she saw there brought her skidding to a halt, her heart stuck in her throat. Five men dressed in black stood near the door, guns in their hands, their faces set in hard, angry lines. A sixth man stood in the middle of the group, his brightly colored shirt and small build setting him apart from the others.

The door flew open again and Hawke strode in, Apirak close behind him. Both men had guns in their hands and dark scowls on their faces. Hawke's eyes glowed light gray and cold, his focus on the brightly dressed man. He said something in Thai, the words more growl than language. The man jumped, turning to face Hawke, words pouring from his mouth in a quick, breathless stream.

For a moment Hawke said nothing, just stared at the man with the same hard look. Then he nodded, gesturing with a hand and stepping back as the black-clad men moved in. They weren't gentle as they urged the sixth man up the stairs, their booted feet pounding against the floor.

In the wake of their departure, the foyer fell silent, the tension thick. Miranda spoke into it, anxious to know what was going on. "Did you find your brother?"

Hawke's cold gaze focused on her and she resisted the urge to take a step back. "No, but we're going to."

Disappointment and sadness made her step toward him. She touched the rigid muscle of his bicep, wishing she had words that would ease the pain he must be feeling. "I'm sorry."

At her words, his expression softened and he pulled her into a tight hug. "Me, too, but I know where he is. Nothing is going to keep me from bringing him home this time."

"You know this is a trap and you're going to walk right into it." Apirak spoke English and Miranda wondered if he did it purposely to pull her into an argument she had a feeling had been going on for a while.

"What's going on?" She pulled back from Hawke's arms, trying to read the truth in his face.

"We found Sharee where he said he would be, but my brother wasn't with him. A little encouragement and he was able to tell us where he left Simon."

"Left him?"

"Austin gave him instructions to keep Simon alive until he had the documents in hand, but to not let us near each other. Simon's in a warehouse in Mae Hong Son. I'm going to get him."

"Austin will be waiting for you. And he won't be alone." Apirak spoke again, his frustration obvious.

"Sharee wasn't alone, either, and we were fine."

"Sharee is a fool. Austin is not."

"Anyone who does what he has done is a fool." Hawke dropped the pack he was carrying.

"And going up against him alone isn't foolish as well?"

"Alone?" Miranda interrupted the argument, not liking what she was hearing.

"It's the only way to make sure no one knows I'm coming. The only way to keep Simon from being killed."

"You're not the only one able to move quietly and quickly, Hawke." Apirak dropped his own pack on the floor, his jaw set.

"Which is easier to spot, my friend, one tiger lurking in the grass or two?" Hawke's tone was almost gentle and Miranda knew he understood his friend's worry. Just as she knew he didn't plan to let it stop him.

"Tigers hunt alone."

"Exactly. I'm going into the warehouse and I'm getting my brother. I want you here with Sharee until someone from the Royal Thai police comes to collect him."

"You've got five men guarding him. You do not need one more. The truth is, you know you are probably walking into a death trap and you refuse to bring any of us with you."

Hawke didn't deny it and Miranda went cold with the truth of what Apirak had said. "Hawke—"

"Call Jack, Apirak. He's on his way to Mae Hong Son. Tell him that I'm headed to the old warehouse south of town. He'll know it. If anything happens, you've got the documents. Make sure he gets them."

"You should wait for him to arrive and go together," Miranda tried again, but Hawke seemed determined to ignore her protest.

"I can't waste any more time. I've got to go." He turned to his friend. "I'm trusting you to take care of Miranda while I'm gone. However long that might be."

He was asking for more than a few hours or even a few days. He was asking a man Miranda didn't know to protect her for as long as was necessary; to take responsibility for her life if he could no longer do it.

But her life was her responsibility and Miranda had no intention of staying safe in Hawke's compound while he walked into danger alone.

She thought about arguing with him, but knew she wouldn't change his mind. She'd let him leave and then she'd find a way to follow.

Apirak's jaw tightened, his eyes flashed, but it seemed he, too, had given up the argument. "You are a brother to me. Of course, I will do as you request."

Hawke nodded, then pushed open the door. "I'll be back as soon as I have Simon."

Miranda thought he'd walk away without another word, but his gaze swept from Doom to Apirak and finally came to rest on her. "Stay with Apirak."

"I will." For as long as it took for her to find a ride into town.

"Promise me, Miranda." His gray eyes speared into hers.

He knew. She was sure of it. He'd seen her plan written on her face or in her eyes and he wanted to keep her from following through on it.

Too bad. She wasn't promising anything. "You'd better go. Your brother needs you."

"Babe, I'm not going anywhere until I have your word you'll stay with Apirak. Every minute you refuse to give it is another minute Simon is in the hands of brutal men who have no conscience that can't be bought."

He knew her too well. Miranda couldn't imagine

how that was possible after so few days of knowing each other, but he did and he'd called her bluff.

She swallowed back her protest, threw her arms around his waist, holding him tight for just a moment, feeling his warm strength and vibrant life.

And she couldn't imagine going back to a life without him in it.

"Be careful, Hawke."

"You know I will."

"Then I'll promise to stay with Apirak, but I'm not happy about it."

He tilted her chin, staring down into her face, a soft smile playing at the corners of his mouth. "You don't have to worry about me, babe. You know that faith you were talking about? I've finally found it and one way or another, I'm thinking I'll be just fine."

With that, he placed a gentle kiss on her lips and walked away.

Apirak pulled the door closed, his stiff shoulders and angry scowl telling Miranda just how unhappy he was to be left behind.

"Do you think he'll be okay?" She knew there was no answer to the question, but asked it anyway.

"I think I would be happier if I were going with him."

"We need to call Jack. Maybe he'll be able to get there with some agents."

"He won't bring any agents in with him. Too big a show of force and Simon will be killed outright. It is better for a few highly trained men to go in."

"But not one?"

"No," he shook his head, "Hawke never would have allowed any of us to go in alone. He goes himself, though, to protect his men and his brother."

"But what does any of that matter if Hawke and Simon don't have a chance?"

"They have a chance. They'd have more of one if I could be there. Come," Apirak took her arm and led her into a large office. "I need to call McKenzie."

He picked up the phone, dialing a number he must have memorized. While he spoke, Miranda paced the room, restless energy shivering along her spine and demanding she take action. Prayers flitted through her mind, barely coalescing before they took flight. There had to be something she could do besides hide away in the house waiting for Hawke and his brother to be murdered.

No, there wasn't. She'd given her word to stay close to Apirak.

To stay close to him.

Miranda's heart skipped a beat, then accelerated. She'd given her word to stay close to Hawke's friend. She hadn't given her word to stay in the compound. Should she try to get Apirak to take her to the warehouse?

Lord, I don't know what You want me to do. Please, give me some idea of what path I should take. The prayer whispered from the deepest part of her soul. Making a mistake, doing the wrong thing, could quite possibly get her and several men killed. And doing nothing might mean Hawke and Simon's death.

There had been so many times in her life when she'd hesitated, so many times when she'd missed opportunities and blessings because she was afraid to trust God's ability to steer her course.

This would not be one of those times. In her heart, she knew she had to go after Hawke. For now, that was all that mattered.

She'd waited until Apirak hung up the phone and then she set to work convincing him that her plan was a much more reasonable one than Hawke's.

TWENTY-TWO

Hawke felt the cool metal of the gun he'd pulled from its holster and the soft kiss of mist pressing against his skin, but only as periphery sensations. His focus was on the warehouse that sat in the midst of overgrown grass and overflowing garbage bags. Years ago, he'd played here with friends, exploring the building with both fear and exhilaration, the empty warehouse too tempting for the children to ignore. Then, as now, the building held an air of secrecy, the mist drifting over the empty parking lot and the fields that surrounded it making it seem haunted and lonely. If Simon was there, Sharee's men would be there, as well. And Hawke had no reason to doubt Sharee's word on the matter. The man was a coward. Without men and guns to back him up, he'd caved, sputtering places and names with abandon, confirming Hawke's belief that Austin had set up Simon's kidnapping and insisting Hawke's brother was still alive.

Hawke prayed the second part was as true as the first. He hadn't expected Simon to be in the village, but his disappointment had still been real. Now he was counting on finding Simon in the bowels of an abandoned warehouse. If his brother wasn't there, Hawke would keep searching, keep questioning until he found him.

For now, he'd focus on this moment, this goal.

He eased toward the building on his belly, using thick mist and shifting shadows to hide his movements, his gut screaming for him to hurry, his mind insisting he continue the slow, plodding pace. The area surrounding the warehouse offered plenty of cover. The parking lot and open fields that use to resound with activity and motion had been abandoned years ago and were now filled with debris and car carcasses.

Hawke used the refuse to his advantage, slithering behind piles of garbage and rusted vehicles until he was close enough to see inside the broken windows. He stayed there watching, waiting for any sign the warehouse was occupied. It came within minutes, a dark figure passing in front of the broken glass. A sloppy move. One that could cost a man his life. Minutes later, a guard moved around the side of the building, careless and at ease. Which meant the element of surprise was still with Hawke.

He waited until the man turned the next corner, then moved up behind him, knocking him out with the butt of his gun and catching his body before it could hit the ground. Now he moved quickly around the back of the building, his senses on high alert, his body humming with adrenaline.

The back of the warehouse was clear of guards and he moved to a window there, pulling a cutting tool from his belt and using it to remove the glass. Noise drifted from deep inside the old building, muted voices and laughter that set Hawke's teeth on edge. Sharee's men laughed while Simon suffered, but it wouldn't be for long.

Hawke eased into the dark room beyond the window, the scent of decay and the musty odor of age hitting him in the face. He ignored it, concentrating his attention on the voices and laughter, straining to hear any sound of approaching footsteps as he tried to picture the building's layout in his mind. Offices along the back wall, a hallway that led out into the open part of the warehouse and an upper level that housed a kitchen, dining area and one more office. If Hawke was keeping a hostage that would be the place he'd do it, not on the lower level where escape would be easy. There were two sets of stairs—one off the main warehouse area, the other at the end of the hallway outside the door.

Hawke eased the door open, peering out into the dark hallway. Nothing moved and the voices remained muted. Sharee's men were as foolish as their leader. He moved silently, the carpeted floor making soundless movement easy. The stairwell was empty, the darkness above suggesting that the upstairs was empty, too. Hawke took the stairs two at a time, pausing at the top, listening to the silence. From here, the voices were almost inaudible, the hollow empty feel of the upstairs hallway doing nothing to ease Hawke's alert state.

The hair on the back of his neck stood up, his nerves humming a warning. Something was wrong. As much as he believed Sharee's men to be fools, they wouldn't leave a prisoner without a guard. Either Simon wasn't here, or they were so confident he couldn't be freed, they had nothing to worry about.

Either was bad news and Hawke moved with

caution, peering into the open doorway that led into the employee cafeteria. There was little left there. A few chairs, a table, layers of dust and rat droppings that showed no sign of having been walked through recently. The kitchen was the same, empty, layered in dust, the smell of old food still hanging in the air.

The office was at the end of the hall, the door closed, no sounds coming from beyond it. It wasn't locked, and Hawke knew that if Simon were inside, he wouldn't be alone. He pushed it open anyway, knowing that was his only choice.

"I thought you'd be here sooner. I guess I gave you more credit than you deserve." The voice was smooth as honey, the man who stood on the other side of the door tall, lanky, with blond hair and deep brown eyes.

Austin. Hawke recognized him from the pictures he'd seen at the apartment. "And I thought someone who worked for the DEA would have more honor than to sell secrets to the Wa."

"What is honor worth? Not much in today's market." Austin smirked. "Put your gun down, Morran. I wouldn't want your brother to get hurt after you took the time to come save him." He gestured to the left, and Hawke caught sight of his brother. Seated in a metal folding chair, his hands tied behind his back, his feet tied to the chair legs, he looked haggard, bruised and as cantankerous as ever.

"Like I said before, it took you long enough, bro." Simon's voice was raspy and he winced as he spoke, his normally tan skin pale beneath the bruises.

"I was trying to give you plenty of time to escape on your own. I didn't want your youthful self-esteem to be injured by having to have me rescue you." As he spoke,

Hawke took stock of the two men who stood on either side of Simon. Both were armed and built like fighters.

"I hate to cut this touching reunion short, but you've got something I want. Hand it over now before I lose what little patience I have left."

"Let my brother go. Then the papers are yours."

"You don't hold all the cards this time, Morran. I do. Now, drop your weapon and give me the documents." Austin nodded toward one of the men, his dark eyes flashing as the man put a gun to Simon's head.

"Don't do it, bro."

The man slammed a fist into Simon's head and Hawke lunged forward, ready to do battle for his brother. The click of a gun safety froze him. The barrel of the man's gun pressed into the soft flesh beneath Simon's jaw. And Hawke had no choice but to place his gun on the floor and wait for Austin's next move.

Convincing Apirak to bring her to the warehouse had taken less effort than Miranda had imagined it would. Now they were heading toward the town of Mae Hong Son, the morning mist drifting in lazy patches across the road. The sky had darkened in the time since Hawke had left, golden dawn replaced by bleak, gray clouds. It seemed an ominous warning. Was she making a mistake? Should she have stayed in Hawke's compound? She asked herself the same questions over and over again as Apirak maneuvered through narrow streets and dim alleys. Finally, he pulled the motorcycle to a stop and climbed off. "You stay here. I'll go find Hawke and Simon."

"No way. We're supposed to stick together, and that's exactly what we're going to do." Miranda scrambled off after him, nerves making her stomach twist and churn.

"Lady, this is not a game. This is real danger. Men with guns are going to try to kill us both if we give them a chance."

"Sounds exactly like the past few days. I'll feel right at home."

Apirak shot her a look, his dark eyes reflecting nothing of what he felt. "Hawke will have my hide if I bring you into that warehouse."

"Hawke's going to have *both* our hides for coming out here." Rain began to fall in light drops that ran down Miranda's cheeks and splattered her T-shirt. She brushed drops from her forehead and hurried to keep up with Apirak. She didn't know where the warehouse was located, knew nothing about the small town she was hurrying through and had no desire to get lost in it.

"With good reason. He's trying to keep you safe. Bringing you here isn't going to accomplish that."

"But we're doing it, so let's just get over the fact that I'm going to be in danger and get this done."

Apirak shot her another glance, this time something like amusement glowing in the depth of his gaze. "I can see why Hawke enjoys being around you."

"He doesn't enjoy it. He feels he has no choice."

"Because you saved his life. So he told me, but I don't think that's the only reason. Come on—" he grabbed her elbow and pulled her into a narrow alley "—the warehouse is just outside of town."

"Do you think Jack is already there?"

"I wish I did. He was a half hour out when we spoke."

"We could call in the police."

"Not yet. The police go running in there with guns drawn and people will die. We can't risk that one of those people will be Hawke or Simon."

"So we're going in there alone?"

"*I* am going in there alone. *You* are staying outside and staying hidden."

"But—"

"Do you have a gun?"

"No."

"Know how to use one?"

"No, but—"

"Then the only thing you can do is get in the way." They stepped out of the alley and crossed a field of knee-deep grass. In the distance, mist danced around a brick building, touching piles of trash and beat-up old clunkers that were parked nearby.

"That's it. The warehouse. We've got to move in slow and stay close to the ground. I'll find you a safe spot when we get nearer. Ready?"

"As I'll ever be." Which wasn't saying much. As far as Miranda was concerned a life of intrigue and danger was something she could do without.

"Then let's go." Apirak moved forward, hunching down so that the long grass partially hid him. Between that and the heavy mist, he became almost invisible, his silent movements causing him to blend effortlessly with his surroundings. Miranda's own movements were more awkward, her hunched, sliding shuffle producing too much noise and motion. If anyone were watching from the warehouse, they'd see her for sure.

She could only pray no one was watching.

With every step, the warehouse came into sharper

focus—worn bricks, broken windows, a parking lot half full of broken-down cars—it seemed a lonely abandoned place. If people were in it, there was no evidence. No cars, no lights, nothing that would indicate occupancy.

She and Apirak approached from the front, a double-wide door and dangling faded sign indicating the entrance. They were a few hundred yards away when the door banged open. Before Miranda could react, she was on the ground, Apirak pressing her down into moist grass and earth. "Stay here. I've got to see what's happening."

He crept away before she could respond, slithering like a snake toward the building. For a moment, Miranda felt disorientated, not sure if she should do as he said, slink back the way they'd come or move forward. She levered up just a little, saw several men moving out of the building. She caught a glimpse of dark clothes and guns, and felt the same sense of determination she'd felt the night she'd met Hawke. She hadn't been able to turn her back when he was a stranger. Nor could she do it now.

Slowly, one soft slide after another, she moved toward the warehouse and the men.

TWENTY-THREE

Timing was everything. Hawke knew it. And so he waited, letting Austin and his men take his weapon, search him for the documents and then force him outside, his hands tied behind his back, Simon shuffling along beside him. The procession moved toward an old jeep that looked as junky as any of the other vehicles abandoned in the parking lot, the tension in the air as thick as the morning mist.

"Those documents better be in your car, Morran." Austin's face and neck were flushed with irritation and anger, but there was worry in his eyes and a sheen of sweat on his brow. Time was running out and he knew it.

"We'll find out soon enough, won't we?" Hawke kept his voice bland, not willing to be pulled into the other man's emotion. If he were going to get his brother out of this alive, he needed a cool head and quick reflexes. A little divine help wouldn't hurt, either. *Lord, I know I'm coming to You a little late in my life and I know I've made a lot of mistakes, but I finally believe what my parents told me. I finally believe You gave everything up for me and I'm ready and willing to give it all up for You. If this is the end for me, I'm prepared, but please don't let it be the end for Simon. Help me get him out of this alive.*

He said the prayer quickly, his muscles tensing as one of Austin's men shoved Simon into the Jeep. This was it. The time to make his move. And it better be a good one.

A sweep of his foot brought Austin down. A swing of Hawke's bound wrists to his neck kept him there. Hawke spun, lifting his arms to block the blow one of Sharee's men was aiming his way. His wrist went numb, but he ignored it and swung for the man's face, hearing the satisfying crunch of bone against bone.

Someone shouted, the words not registering as Hawke slammed his knee into another man's stomach. Simon was out of the Jeep now, head-butting a third man. If they could get a gun, get the keys to the Jeep, they just might have a chance.

More men poured from the warehouse. Ten, maybe more. Hawke tried not to think of the odds stacked against him.

"Find the keys, Simon. We need to get out of here!" He shouted the words as he reached for Austin's fallen gun. A volley of shots and the ground near his feet exploded. He dove for cover, rolling under the Jeep, his gaze searching for Simon and finding him crouching behind a pile of garbage.

"Get out of here, kid. They won't shoot me. Not until they have what they want, but they've got no qualms about doing away with you."

"No way, bro. If we go down, we go down together."

"Then let's both get out of here. If we can't get the Jeep, maybe we can outrun them." It was hopeless.

Hawke knew it, but trying for freedom was better than sitting and waiting for recapture. "On the count of three." He met Simon's eyes, saw his own hopelessness and determination reflected there.

"One. T—"

Another barrage of bullets followed the first, this time coming from the behind Hawke. He glanced back, saw Jack McKenzie and three other men crouched down and moving in.

"Move, Morran. We'll cover you."

Hawke didn't wait for another invitation. He met Simon's gaze again. Nodded. And ran.

This was as close to war as Miranda ever hoped to get. From her vantage point behind a garbage can, she watched as several of Sharee's men fell to the ground. The rest dove for cover, firing shots wildly as they went. Hawke and a dark-haired young man were running toward Jack McKenzie. They wove and zig-zagged, bullets flying too close for comfort as they went. Apirak had disappeared at the first sound of gunfire, slipping into mist and shadows. Miranda imagined he was slipping closer to Sharee's people, hoping to get a clearer shot.

She, on the other hand, was cowering behind garbage and praying for all she was worth. It seemed the battle went on for an eternity, gunfire being exchanged, shouts and groans and a harsh metallic scent hanging in the air. Then, as quickly as it started, it ended, the world falling silent. Not even a bird or a chirping cricket breaking the stillness.

In the silence, Miranda could hear every beat of her heart, feel the mad pulsing of her terror. She wanted to run, but had no idea who had won the battle or if it had been won at all. Had no idea which direction she should go if she decided to run. Toward the building? Away from it?

She slid down on her belly, slowly, cautiously moving backward, sure that at any moment her movement would attract attention and bullets would fly once again. Something wrapped around her ankle and Miranda jumped, barely stifling a scream as she scrambled to her knees, pivoting to face her attacker.

The dark hair, scarred face and quick-silver eyes were so familiar Miranda felt as if she'd been seeing them every day for years. She scrambled to her feet, relief coursing through her. "Hawke."

"Didn't you give your word that you'd stay with Apirak?" Hawke growled the words, his irritation obvious.

Miranda didn't care. She was so glad he was okay— that at least for now they were safe—that she lurched toward him, wrapping her arms around his waist, clinging tight, sure she would be happy to stay that way forever. "Is it over?"

"Close. Jack and his men are cleaning things up, trying to pull Sharee's men out of any holes they might be hiding in. So—" he leaned back so he could look down at her "—we were discussing the fact that you broke your word."

"Actually, I didn't. Apirak is here."

"It's true." Apirak stepped into view. "We came together."

"As if that makes it a good thing." Hawke scowled, but there was a lightness to his expression that Miranda hadn't seen before, a peace that emanated from him.

"Your brother is okay?" Miranda asked the question, though she was sure she already knew the answer. Hawke wouldn't be so relaxed if his brother was injured or in danger.

"Simon is good." Hawke wrapped his arm around Miranda's shoulder as if he didn't want to let her out of his sight again. "There he is. With Jack." Hawke gestured to the man Miranda had seen running beside him before the battle began.

"He's young."

"Thirteen years younger than me. Come meet him." He led her toward the other men, his stride easy and unhurried, as if he had all the time in the world. Maybe he did. He was home now. Safe. And soon Miranda would be returning home, as well. The thought brought a sadness she hadn't expected to feel. She swallowed it back as she greeted Simon and Jack. Sirens sounded in the distance and a police car raced into sight, pulling into the parking lot, a marked truck following close behind it. Men leaped from the vehicles and fanned out to cuff and escort men to the waiting transportation.

This was it then. The truth would be revealed. She and Hawke would be cleared. Life would go on the way it always had. Except that Justin wouldn't be in it. And she would never be the same. Her loss, the things she'd been through, seemed carved into the very fiber of her being. She leaned against an old car, listening as the men spoke, their words flowing over her in strangely comforting waves.

Until chaos broke out again. A gunshot, a shout, a police officer falling to the ground.

"I don't want any trouble," a tall, thin American spoke, his face swollen and splattered with blood, his voice empty of emotion, a gun held to the head of the police officer who stood in front of him.

"It's too late for that, Austin." Jack spoke quietly, a weariness in his tone that Miranda thought must come from facing someone once trusted and now proven untrustworthy.

"I've hurt no one, Jack. Not yet. And I don't plan to. Just give me some time to talk to my wife and kids. Then I'll turn myself in." As lies went, this one wasn't convincing, the words of a desperate man and nothing more.

"I think you know it doesn't work that way. Put the gun down. Killing a man won't accomplish your goals."

"But it will buy me some time." He pulled the trigger, firing past the officer as he moved backward, the shot landing several feet away. The rest seemed to happen in slow motion. Standing beside Hawke and Apirak, Jack pulled his gun. All of their focus was on Austin. Miranda's own gaze was trained in that direction, but something drew her attention, a subtle shifting in the air, a warning of danger that had her turning. A man lurched up from the tall grass, a gun drawn and pointed at the nearest target.

"Simon! Watch out!" Miranda yelled the warning, hurled herself toward the young man, pushing him out of the way.

Something slammed into her chest, throwing her backward, stealing her breath. She gasped, trying for air that wouldn't come, something hot and thick sliding down her arm. She tried to wipe it away, but couldn't move, her body weighted and pressing ever deeper into the welcoming earth.

The sound of more gunfire came as if from a

distance, dull reports that danced at the edge of Miranda's conscience. Her eyes drifted closed, but she forced them open, trying to turn her head to see if Simon was okay.

"Babe!" Hawke was there, kneeling beside her, his face pale, his expression stark and raw.

"Simon…"

"Is fine. Don't talk, okay?"

"I'm fine." Or maybe not. Her vision blurred, her head swam and darkness pressed in on her. She kept her eyes open, afraid to let go, afraid of what would happen if she did.

"I said don't talk. You're bleeding. This is going to hurt." He pressed against her shoulder and the pain she hadn't felt exploded through her, stealing the light. This time, she didn't fight it.

TWENTY-FOUR

It hurt to breathe. That was Miranda's first thought. The second came as she opened her eyes. She was alive.

"Miranda?" The voice was familiar, but not the one she must have been subconsciously hoping for. She turned her head, meeting Lauren's bright blue eyes.

"Lauren. Am I back home?" No. That didn't make sense. She was in a hospital, a television running monotonous, unintelligible tones.

"You're in Bangkok. You were flown here five days ago. I came as soon as I was called. Max is here, too. He's gone to get coffee. We've been worried sick about you. Why didn't you tell me the truth, Miranda? How could you let me think you were a criminal?" Lauren sniffed, but there were no tears in her eyes. Nor was there concern or any of the other things Miranda might have hoped for.

"I tried to tell you. You chose not to believe me." Her throat hurt and she was desperate for the water she could see sitting on the table beside her bed. She tried to reach for it, but the simple movement sent pain shooting through her shoulder and chest.

"You could have tried harder, Miranda. All those

interviews I had with the press, telling them that you were just confused, that you'd been pulled in by a man more worldly than you." She shook her head, bit her too-perfect lips. "I look like a fool."

"Sorry." Miranda had no energy to say anything more, and she closed her eyes to block out the sight of her sister.

"You're not going back to sleep before Max gets back, are you? He's been beside himself with worry."

Miranda forced her eyes open again, saw that Lauren was peering down at her. "At least one of you was."

"You're not implying that I wasn't worried?"

"Of course not, Lauren."

"I know you've been through a lot, but I don't think that gives you the right to be snooty."

Miranda responded with a question she'd wanted to ask since she'd opened her eyes. "Where's Hawke?"

"Hawke? The man with the scar, you mean?"

"Hawke."

"I sent him away. Max and I thought seeing him would bring back bad memories."

"Sent him away? When?"

"Five or six times since I got here. I'm hoping this time it sticks. He's not your type, Miranda. You know that, don't you?"

"How would you know what my type is?" The question slipped out and Miranda was glad. Her pain was increasing by the minute, her throat hot and tight. She wanted to ask for a drink of water, but opted for feigning sleep instead. Better to ignore Lauren than to fight with her.

She heard a door open, knew it must be Max returning, but didn't have any desire to see even him, her pain becoming so intense, her fatigue so overwhelming, she didn't have the energy to even open her eyes.

"She woke up for a minute, but went right back under. I still think we should transfer her home now. She'll get better faster there." Lauren's words seemed muffled, her inflections oddly out of sync.

"You know she's not stable enough for that, Laur. Did you tell her I was here?"

"Yes. She seemed less than impressed."

"What do you expect? She's been through three surgeries…." His words faded away as the pain dragged Miranda back under.

When she surfaced again, the room was silent but for the quiet beep and hum of machinery. Miranda's pain crested and receded with every breath she took. She tried to open her eyes, but her lids seemed fused together, all her effort not producing even the slightest movement. Panic beat a hard fast rhythm in her chest, each beat of her heart only adding to the pain. She wanted to scream, but her vocal chords seemed paralyzed, her body refusing to respond to any of her commands. The slow beep of the machine accelerated and Miranda wondered if she'd die here, frozen in place, unable to call for help.

A warm hand pressed against her forehead, the touch so comforting tears slipped from her eyes. If she were going to die, at least she wouldn't be alone.

"No more tears, babe. My heart is already broken enough."

Hawke. Miranda tried again to open her eyes, focusing on the gentle brush of his hands against her cheek. Finally she managed it, the effort making her queasy. The room was dimly lit, the television off,

Hawke's rugged face bent close to hers, the shadow of a beard covering his jaw.

"There you are. I was wondering when I'd look in those beautiful eyes again." He spoke quietly, setting a book down on the table and grabbing a cup with a straw sticking out of it. "Here. Take a sip."

She did, the icy water easing some of the burning in her throat, though it did little to ease her pain. "Thank you."

But more tears slipped out, sliding into her hair, dripping into her ears.

"Shh." Hawke wiped the tears away, his hand a butterfly kiss against her skin. "Are you in pain?"

"Yes."

"Here. Press this and the pain will be gone before you know it." He put her thumb over a small button.

Miranda didn't even ask what it was, or what it would do to her. She just wanted every breath to stop being agony.

Within minutes the pain eased to a dull ache, her tense body finally relaxing.

"There. You already look more comfortable." Hawke brushed a hand along her shoulder and down her arm, gently cupping her hand in his. "Your sister said you woke earlier. Didn't she tell you about the morphine pump?"

"She was too busy telling me what an inconvenience I've been to her. Where is she? And Max? Isn't he here, too?" Miranda's throat was burning again, an aching dryness that she couldn't ignore. "Can I have some more water?"

He nodded, held the cup while she sipped again, his eyes silvery gray and filled with emotion Miranda couldn't name. "Your family is at their hotel. I convinced them it would be for the best if they got some rest. Would you like me to call them? They're close. It won't take long for them to come."

She shook her head. "I'd like to see Max, but I can't handle Lauren right now."

"You don't have to handle anything, babe. I'll handle it for you." He spoke in smooth soothing tones designed to comfort and Miranda let herself be drawn into them, her muscles relaxing, her head easing back onto the pillow.

"How is your brother?"

"Simon is great. He's been here several times and is anxious to thank you for saving his life."

"And Austin?"

"He's recovering from several gunshot wounds. He'll live, but I'm not sure he's going to be happy about it."

"Did he confess?"

"Not at first, but once Jack threatened to hand him over to the Thai authorities, he was more willing to talk. He admitted that he'd been in the Wa's pocket for years, almost from the day he'd arrived in Thailand. That he passed on information about me to Green."

"He must have known he'd eventually get caught."

"Maybe he did. Maybe he didn't care. His cause was everything. He'd reconnected with his birth mother and her father years after he was adopted and was brought into his grandfather's militant philosophy. When his grandfather died, Austin took up his cause. A few months after he arrived in Thailand, Sharee offered him big money to be the Wa's informant. He agreed and has been sending money to Chechnya ever since."

"And Green? Liam?"

"Both have been arrested. Neither will admit to anything, but there's enough evidence to convict them."

"And Randy?"   •

Hawke shook his head and squeezed her hand. "He's disappeared. I don't think he'll ever be found."

"You think he's dead?"

"Yeah. I do. Liam and Green would have seen him as the weak link. Getting rid of him would have assured his silence."

"I hope you're wrong. I hope he's alive somewhere and that the police find him. I hate to think of him being murdered."

"Then don't think about it. Think about getting better." He brushed strands of hair from her cheek, his fingers lingering there.

"I guess this means the police aren't after you anymore. You're finally in the clear. I'm so glad."

"I told you before you didn't have to worry about me, but I think I'm starting to like it." He smiled and Miranda's heart filled with an emotion she didn't want to name. One she hadn't wanted to feel. But it was there, as real as the man sitting beside her, as real as the connection between them that had become stronger with each passing day, each passing moment.

"Hawke—"

He pressed a finger against her lips. "Enough talking for now. You've got to rest so you can heal."

"I've been resting for five days."

"Five days isn't nearly long enough, babe. You almost died in Mae Hong Son. They airlifted you here once you were stabilized. Performed surgery to repair your lung. Had to go back in twice more to stop internal bleeding. It's been a tough few days. Now that you're awake, things are looking up. Let's keep it that way."

"I don't remember anything about what happened." Except the pain. And Hawke. He seemed to be part of all her memories, all her thoughts, and having him here made the world seem much more right than it had when she'd opened her eyes to find Lauren. "But I know I'm glad you're here." The words slipped out and she didn't wish them back.

"And I'm glad *you're* here." Hawke leaned in, pressing a tender kiss to her lips. "I thought we were going to lose you."

"I guess I'm tougher than you thought."

"You're exactly what I thought—a sweet, strong, funny woman who cares just a little too much about everyone. Meeting you has changed me, Miranda. For the better. I want you to know that."

He was going to say goodbye. Miranda knew it and she fought unwelcome tears at the thought. She'd known from the very beginning that they were from different worlds, that they had nothing in common. "Are you leaving now?"

"Leaving? Babe, I'll stay here for the rest of my life if you want me to." He grinned, but there was a seriousness to his voice that made Miranda's heart jump.

"The rest of your life might be a long time."

"The rest of my life won't be nearly long enough if I get to spend it with you."

"Hawke—"

"I know this isn't the time to discuss it, but every time you were wheeled into surgery, I prayed that God would give me the opportunity to tell you what an important part of my life you've become."

"I feel the same."

"Then maybe when you're feeling better and finally get out of here, we can spend time doing what normal couples do—dinner, movies, walks on the beach."

"As opposed to running from drug dealers, racing through the jungle and getting shot?"

"Exactly."

"I'd like that. I'd like that a lot."

Hawke smiled again, lifting her hand, kissing her knuckles, his lips warm against her flesh, his eyes promising all the things she'd thought she'd never have. "Me, too. But first, healing. How's the pain?"

"Better. I can't even tell where I was shot." Miranda glanced down, trying to find bandages, but a blanket was pulled up to her shoulders and she could see nothing.

"A few inches below your collarbone. The bullet missed your heart, but went through your lung and out your back. The doctors say you are very lucky to be alive. I say you are very blessed."

"A week ago, I'm not sure if I would have agreed. Now, I know you're right. It was so hard to lose Justin. For a while I was sure God had turned His back on me. He didn't, though. He was there for me. And He'll keep being there. I know that now."

"I understand. I've spent ten years looking for justice only to realize that justice is for God to mete out. Not me. I've quit my job with the DEA and I'm selling my portion of the business to my brother. He plans to stay here."

"And you?"

"I'm going to Virginia. My friend Noah told me a year ago that he had a job for me if I ever wanted one. I'll be training service dogs."

"That's wonderful."

"Yeah, it is. A new life. A new home. And something that appeals to me even more."

"What's that?" Her heart thumped a slow, thick rhythm as she looked into his eyes.

"I'll only be a few hours away from a woman I can't imagine living life without."

Miranda smiled, her eyes drifting closed, sleep wanting to steal her away again. A thought floated on the edge of dreams and she forced her eyes open, looked into Hawke's eyes. "I'm getting tired of living in Essex."

"Are you?"

"Yes. And I can open a bakery just about anywhere."

"Where are you thinking would be a good place?"

"Somewhere close to you."

Hawke's smile lit his face. He leaned toward her, gently pulling her into his arms and the emotion Miranda hadn't wanted to name welled up inside, the word for it dancing through her head and in her heart until she couldn't deny it any longer. "I love you, Hawke."

"You know what, babe? I love you, too."

EPILOGUE

"You really don't intend to live here?" Lauren's voice was high pitched, her blue eyes, framed by stylish glasses, scanned the small living room she and Miranda were standing in.

"Actually, I do." Miranda lifted a box from the floor, wincing a little as the muscles in her chest and back pulled against scar tissue.

"But it's…" Lauren looked around the little bungalow Miranda had purchased a week after her return from Thailand. It had taken another few weeks to finalize the sale of her bakery to an employee who'd jumped at the chance to own it. The town house had also been easy to sell. Now, after a month of nervous anticipation, moving day had arrived. Unfortunately, Lauren had felt the need to be part of it and had followed Miranda's Saturn and the moving truck and crew she'd hired, her Mercedes crammed with boxes of Miranda's belongings.

"It's what?" Miranda glanced around the cozy room—the gleaming hardwood floors, the muted yellow paint, the windows that lined the front wall and looked out onto the blue-green water of Smith Mountain Lake.

"Small. Old."

"I think it's cute and homey."

"Which just shows how confused you are. Miranda, this is just a bad idea all around. You've fallen for a man who isn't right for you. That's bad enough. But to move hundreds of miles from home to be near him. That's insane. Obviously you still haven't recovered from your injury."

"The injury was to my lung, not my brain." Miranda pulled a pile of books out of the box and placed them on one of the built-in bookshelves that flanked the fireplace. The clock on the mantel said twelve-thirty. When she'd spoken to Hawke the previous night, she'd told him she'd be at the house by noon. He'd said he would be there to meet her. She'd counted on it. Now disappointment beat a sullen pulse behind her eyes, the headache she'd been fighting off during the five-hour drive from Maryland slamming full-force through her skull.

She pulled another pile of books from the box, shooting a look at her sister as she did so and gesturing toward the partially open front door. "Why don't you head to the airport, Lauren? You wouldn't want to miss your flight."

"I've got hours before it takes off. Besides, I've been thinking of canceling the photo shoot."

Miranda knew that wasn't the truth, but she played the game anyway. "Why?"

"Because you obviously need me here. I'd hoped that Max could leave his job for a week and come stay with you, but he just refused to take more time off."

"He refused because he'd already stayed with me in

Essex for two weeks. I wanted him to get back to his life, so I told him I'd be fine on my own. And I am." She dropped the empty box, lifted another one and froze as a short, sharp rap sounded on the door. It swung open the rest of the way, a tall, dark figure filling the doorway.

"I knew if I was a few minutes late you'd get into trouble." Hawke's gravely voice was so familiar, so welcome, tears filled Miranda's eyes.

"I'm not getting into trouble. I'm unpacking."

"And I think that was exactly what I told you not to do." He strode forward, took the box from her hands, a gentle smile softening the harsh planes and angles of his face. He'd left his hair down and it fell forward, brushing against Miranda's skin as he leaned down to capture her lips in a searing kiss.

"Excuse me, but you're not alone, you know." Lauren huffed the words and Miranda pulled back, her cheeks heating.

She might have stepped away, but Hawke hooked an arm around her waist and pulled her close. "Do you see that comfortable-looking chair over there?" He pointed to the antique rocker that the movers had brought in a half hour ago. "I want you to sit there and relax while I take care of the rest of these boxes."

"We're doing fine without you, Mr. Morran, and one more person in this room will only make it more claustrophobic. Feel free to leave and come back later after we're done." Lauren's voice was icy cold, her expression haughty.

"I invited Hawke here because I wanted him here, Lauren. And since this is my house, I think I get to decide who stays and who doesn't." Miranda leaned her aching head against Hawke's shoulder and his arm tightened around her waist.

Lauren stiffened, her back ramrod straight and her eyes slitted. "I went out of my way to help you today, Miranda. You act like you don't appreciate it."

"Of course I do, but that's beside the point. You're being rude and you know it. If you can't be more pleasant, you can leave." Miranda's heart broke as she spoke, her dreams of building a relationship with Lauren dying in the face of her sister's inability to think of anyone but herself.

"Obviously, you've decided you don't need family now that *he's* in your life."

"Hawke is the closest family I've ever had."

Lauren blinked and for a moment Miranda thought she'd soften. Then she shrugged, started across the room. "I'm sorry you feel that way. I guess I'll leave you to your *family*." She stepped outside, closing the door firmly behind her.

"Lauren—"

"Let her go, babe. One more word out of her mouth and I was going to throw her out anyway." Hawke spoke quietly,

"I know she's obnoxious, but she's my sister."

"And maybe one day she'll realize it. How two such different women could come from the same family, I don't know." Hawke brushed a hand over Miranda's hair, his fingers tangling in the strands and massaging the base of her neck. "You okay?"

"Better than I was when I arrived and saw that you weren't here."

"Sorry about that, babe. I picked up a surprise for you on my way here and it wasn't cooperating."

"A surprise?" Miranda smiled, easing away from Hawke's arm and turning to face him, her fingers tracing the strong line of his jaw, the ridge of the scar on his cheek. "Did Simon finally decide to visit?"

"Not yet. He's planning to come out in November."

"Then what's the surprise?"

"Sit down and I'll tell you."

"Bribery?"

"Whatever works."

Miranda did as he asked, easing down onto the rocking chair and smiling up at him. "Okay. I did my part. What's the surprise?"

"It's in the car. Wait here and I'll bring it in."

He disappeared out the door and was back moments later, a wiggling, squirming bundle of fur in his arms, the big pink bow tied around its neck sliding and slipping as it moved.

"A puppy!" Miranda reached for the little fur ball, laughing as it licked her chin. "She's adorable. Oh, Hawke, thank you!"

"I thought you might like some company when I couldn't be here."

"You thought I needed a guard dog is more like it." Miranda laughed again, reaching for Hawke's hand, loving the way the solid warmth of it felt.

"Does she look like a guard dog?"

Miranda studied the puppy's brown fur and dark face, her soulful eyes and wagging tail, the pink bow and the shiny gold ring hanging from one end of it.

Shiny gold ring?

Miranda's breath caught in her throat, her hand shaking as she reached out to touch it. A marquis diamond flashed in the overhead light, reflecting all the colors of life, of hope, of dreams fulfilled.

"My friend Noah said I should wait. He said it was too soon to ask you to marry me. But I don't want to wait, babe. Not a year. Not two years. Not somebody else's idea of what a reasonable amount of time is." He knelt down in front of her, his eyes glowing with silver fire. "I love you now. I'll love you tomorrow. I'll love you an eternity from now. So, what do you say?"

"I say your friend doesn't know what he's talking about." Miranda smiled past the tears of joy that were sliding down her cheeks. "I say yes."

Dear Reader,

The world is filled with scary situations. Our faith may be shaken when our prayers seem to go unanswered, or our deepest dreams are never realized. However, true faith is more than believing that God will make everything go our way. It is what Shadrach, Meshach and Abednego had when they said, "If we are thrown into the blazing furnace, the God we serve is able to save us from it… *But even if He does not,* we will not serve your gods." Their faith did not require a miracle. Our faith should be the same. Solid in the face of whatever might come.

This is a truth Miranda Sheldon learns as she is thrust into a situation that might lead to her death. Forced to trust a man she doesn't know, she must believe that whatever happens, God will be there. Join Miranda and Hawke Morran as they journey to Mae Hong Son, Thailand, in search of evidence that will clear their names. What they find there is something neither of them expect, but both desperately need.

All His best,

Shirlee McCoy

QUESTIONS FOR DISCUSSION

1. After her nephew's accident, Miranda prays for God to heal him. When He did not, how did she feel? Were her feelings justified?

2. How does Miranda reconcile her faith with the disappointment and sorrow she feels?

3. Miranda and Hawke are from very different worlds and have very different ideas about life, but they have both experienced loss and heartache. How do those common threads draw them together during the story?

4. From the beginning of the story, Hawke acknowledges God's existence. Why does it take him so long to accept that God has a vested interest in His creation?

5. Hawke has spent years trying to ease the pain of his family's death by fighting against the organization that murdered them, but he's found no comfort in his journey. What is it he is really seeking? How does he find it?

6. Miranda and Hawke both feel guilt and anger about situations they had no control over. Each struggles to understand God's plan and purpose. In the end, what do they learn about God's power, grace and love?

7. When faced with heartbreak and loss, is it difficult to find any good in what we've experienced? Is Miranda able to?

8. Sometimes the path we're on isn't the one God intends us to take. How does Hawke know he's going the wrong direction?

9. Once Hawke decides to change his life, he accepts a job with the DEA. In the end, he learns that even that isn't where God wants him. What is it that God really wants from Hawke? Is Hawke able to give it?

10. Hawke and Miranda seem to have met by chance. By the end of the book, it's clear there was more to their meeting than that. How does the relationship they forge change each of them? How have certain relationships changed *your* life?

Love Inspired®

*C*elebrate Love Inspired's 10th anniversary
with top authors and great stories all year long!

A Tiny Blessings Tale

**Don't judge a person
by appearance alone.**

Life on the mission field
had given Eric a passion
for finding homes for
the world's abandoned
children, but when he
falls for a beautiful model,
will she be able to share
his vision?

Look for

MISSIONARY DADDY
BY
LINDA GOODNIGHT

*Available in August
wherever you buy books.*

REQUEST YOUR FREE BOOKS!
2 FREE RIVETING INSPIRATIONAL NOVELS PLUS 2 FREE MYSTERY GIFTS

Love Inspired®
SUSPENSE

YES! Please send me 2 FREE Love Inspired® Suspense novels and my 2 FREE mystery gifts. After receiving them, if I don't wish to receive any more books, I can return the shipping statement marked "cancel." If I don't cancel, I will receive 4 brand-new novels every month and be billed just $3.99 per book in the U.S. or $4.74 per book in Canada, plus 25¢ shipping and handling per book and applicable taxes, if any*. That's a savings of 20% off the cover price! I understand that accepting the 2 free books and gifts places me under no obligation to buy anything. I can always return a shipment and cancel at any time. Even if I never buy another book from Steeple Hill, the two free books and gifts are mine to keep forever.

123 IDN EL5H   323 IDN ELQH

Name	(PLEASE PRINT)	
Address		Apt. #
City	State/Prov.	Zip/Postal Code

Signature (if under 18, a parent or guardian must sign)

Order online at www.LoveInspiredSuspense.com

Or mail to Steeple Hill Reader Service™:
IN U.S.A.: P.O. Box 1867, Buffalo, NY 14240-1867
IN CANADA: P.O. Box 609, Fort Erie, Ontario L2A 5X3

Not valid to current Love Inspired Suspense subscribers.

**Want to try two free books from another series?
Call 1-800-873-8635 or visit www.morefreebooks.com**

* Terms and prices subject to change without notice. NY residents add applicable sales tax. Canadian residents will be charged applicable provincial taxes and GST. This offer is limited to one order per household. All orders subject to approval. Credit or debit balances in a customer's account(s) may be offset by any other outstanding balance owed by or to the customer. Please allow 4 to 6 weeks for delivery.

Your Privacy: Steeple Hill is committed to protecting your privacy. Our Privacy Policy is available online at www.eHarlequin.com or upon request from the Reader Service. From time to time we make our lists of customers available to reputable firms who may have a product or service of interest to you. If you would prefer we not share your name and address, please check here. ☐

LISUS07

Love Inspired® SUSPENSE

TITLES AVAILABLE NEXT MONTH

Don't miss these four stories in August